DESPERATE MEASURES

MICHAEL REED

RATTLING GOOD YARNS
PRESS

Rattling Good Yarns Press
33490 Date Palm Drive 3065
Cathedral City CA 92235
USA
www.rattlinggoodyarns.com

Cover Design by Rattling Good Yarns Press

Library of Congress Control Number: 2024940883
ISBN: 978-1-955826-63-1

First Edition

Part One

Familial Matters

Chapter 1

Rhonda hadn't fallen down a rabbit hole of fear and anxiety so much as dug the yawning pit herself, one heavy shovelful of angst, terror, and shame at a time. The world churned on, leaving her stranded in a trap of her own making. *We must escape,* for Joey, her beautiful, gay, thirteen-year-old son—if not for herself.

You should have done it years ago.

She stood in the downstairs hallway, staring at the door at the end of the corridor.

"For once in your life, just do it," she whispered to herself. She'd spent the last thirty-five years not doing it—change was hard. But Joey's innocent face flashed in her mind, and that was enough. She took a step, and then another.

Rhonda had longed to escape her angry, menacing father growing up. Beyond that? She'd never imagined what her life would look like. But whatever she might have dreamed, it wasn't this. Her father's angry darkness couldn't hold a candle to her husband, Max.

Out of the frying pan...

She felt as fragile as a tissue paper doll held together by tattered hope. Survived by acrobatic acquiescence to Max's temper and violence, discarding any sense of self. She'd told herself she'd done this for the noble purpose of protecting Joey. But there was nothing heroic about it. It was fear. And it wasn't going to work anymore. Max was planning something. She just knew it, and she'd convinced herself the answer was behind that door.

Meek little Rhonda, Elizabeth would say. *My scared little rabbit.*

Rhonda's sister, Elizabeth, didn't take crap from anyone. Rhonda had never mastered that degree of courage.

She was taking baby steps and should have been sprinting. She prayed there was still time.

There's no way he'll know, she assured herself. *Just go in and look around.* She was alone in the house, Max at work and Joey at school. Fear coursed through her like caustic poison. A burning in her veins. She'd never dared defy Max before. Her nerves thrummed with equal parts exhilaration and terror.

It had been two weeks since Max last hit her or Joey. The anticipation was unbearable, waiting for his slap, his flying fists against her skin.

Frenetic laughter erupted from her throat.

"My husband isn't hitting me. How *suspicious*!"

This is what crazy feels like.

Rhonda walked the length of the hallway before she could talk herself out of it. She slowed near the end, but her mind screamed.

GO!

She passed a mirror on the wall and ignored it. She knew what she'd see. Hazel eyes, wild as a trapped animal. Worry lines etched in her face. Streaks of gray in her shoulder-length auburn hair. The oldest-looking thirty-five-year-old she knew. A face hollowed from years of abuse. *Just like mom.*

Her mother with the dour, haunted expression of a living ghost. Rhonda had become her in all but death.

Her parents died in a single-car accident during Rhonda's first year of college.

Her sister's voice echoed in her head. *My scared little rabbit.*

Elizabeth was fierce, confrontational, and never shied from a fight. Rhonda slinked into her hole and hid from the big, cruel world.

Coward. Not Elizabeth's voice this time, but her own.

Rhonda scanned the door, looking for any sign Max might have rigged it to alert him to someone's trespass, like she'd once seen in an old Robert Redford movie. But there was nothing. His office was off limits. That had always been a sufficient deterrent. Until today.

Max restricted her freedoms and reveled in the dominance. He even forbade her from socializing with the neighbors.

"They stick their noses where they don't belong."

He'd always known when she did. *Maybe he'd installed a camera, like one of those doorbell devices.* She protectively hugged her chest. His punishments were brutal.

She worried about the camera idea.

Before fear could stay her hand, Rhonda reached out and turned the doorknob. The satisfying, *terrifying*, click sent a shiver dancing along her spine. She gave the wooden paneled door a shove. It glided open, revealing the bright, masculinely appointed study beyond.

Max's ergonomic chair sat behind the large wooden desk. A luxurious brown leather sofa against the opposite wall. A couple of oak file cabinets tucked into the corner behind the door. His diplomas and awards from work adorned the white walls. The window in the far wall blazed with cold November sunlight. It glared off the polished hardwood floor. Rhonda shielded her eyes.

Her heart fluttered in rabbit-timid terror as a car slowed out on the road.

Oh God, Max is home!

A moment later the car drove on.

You'll hear the garage door going up, or his keys rattling in the front door. She clearly recalled flipping the doorknob lock *and* the deadbolt, after Joey went out this morning to catch the school bus.

She stepped into the study, heart racing, awed at her boldness.

You did it! Elizabeth would be so proud. Now what? She hadn't a clue what she was looking for, no idea what Max might have secreted away in this lion's den. She just hoped that something would stand out, like a flashing red light—sirens screaming, *this is it!*

There had to be something. Or was she just imagining everything?

No. A man who spit in her face and punched her in the back because she didn't welcome him home with enough gratitude wasn't going to change. A man who smacked his nine-year-old son to the floor, shouting, *"FUCKING FAGGOT!"* because he'd tearfully admitted he'd rather read and garden than play sports, was beyond change. That was during the first pandemic lockdown, and she'd done nothing; dark, shameful memories.

She should have left Max when he first started hitting her, when he'd started hitting Joey for *turning* gay—like anyone with an ounce of intelligence believed anymore that people *turned* gay. But she couldn't bring herself to leave him. Maybe it was the financial security, or just believing this was her lot in life—like her mother. Her excuses were legion and also bullshit. And she knew it. There was no excuse—with one exception. What would Max do if she scraped up enough courage to leave?

Elizabeth was right. Rhonda should never have married Max.

No! Joey came from their union, the joy of her life. He'd come from Max—was the best part of him, apparently the only good Max had to give.

She took a deep calming breath. She listened for the garage door or keys in the deadbolt, but all was quiet—not even any traffic on the road. She eased herself down into Max's chair. Stacks of schematics and official forms covered every inch of the desktop. Max was an engineer, a partner at a prestigious company in DC with a multitude of government contracts.

When nothing on the desk looked unusual—not that she would know, having only a degree in library science—she dug deeper. If there was anything in this house that would tell her what Max was up to, it would be in this room.

It took no time at all. Rhonda checked the center drawer first. It was unlocked. There was a manilla file-folder right on top. In his impeccable handwriting, Max had written on the folder's index tab: *Insurance.* Something deep inside Rhonda's heart shifted, like a brick falling into place, or an axe blade hitting the chopping block.

Maybe it's the house and car insurance. But she knew it wasn't. The folder pulsed with menace. She knew exactly what it was.

But it couldn't be. Max canceled those policies six months ago. "*Too expensive,*" he'd said. "*Besides, the house is paid for, you'll be fine.*"

Rhonda reached into the drawer, heart racing, her skin ice cold. But she didn't lift the folder. Afraid to disturb anything, of leaving any trace that she'd gone through the desk. Everything must remain exactly as he'd left it. She opened the file in situ and stared at the policy statement on top. She noted the date, *November 5*—two weeks ago, and she saw the faux stamp across the page, *Paid*. Rhonda's hand trembled as she flipped the statement to the side and peered down at the cover sheet of the document.

It was over a year and a half ago, right after Max's job promotion. She'd willingly signed the policy and had a physical—apparently, it was illegal to insure someone without his or her consent. It all seemed reasonable. Max was moving up, worth more money—they needed to take precautions.

After Max said he'd canceled the policies, Rhonda forgot about it. You didn't question Max. And he took care of all their finances. She never saw the statements. Shame flooded her like a molten tide of lava. Max hadn't taken her freedom; she'd given it away.

The policy numbers on the statement matched those on the cover letter. Three life insurance policies, one for each of them, for one million dollars each. Still very much active.

Rhonda's face tingled, and her body trembled.

Oh, Max, no.

Chapter 2

"Rhonda, my little rabbit, what's wrong?" Elizabeth's voice was a salve on Rhonda's soul. She'd detested the nickname growing up, but now welcomed the familiar endearment.

After retreating from Max's office, she'd known exactly what to do—call her big sister in West Virginia.

Rhonda held it together. She didn't cry, but she couldn't stop her hands from shaking. She admired her steady, clear voice, though.

"Something's wrong...with Max."

Rhonda cringed at the bark of laughter from her sister. Elizabeth never approved of Max, and Rhonda couldn't blame her. She felt like such a cliché; *the veil finally lifted from my eyes.*

"Sorry," said Elizabeth. Her voice was serious. "What's going on?"

"I found something in his office. Life insurance for all of us. He'd told me six months ago that he canceled the policies. But he lied. They're still active, paid up." Rhonda wasn't sure she'd conveyed the gravity of the situation, her suspicions.

"Okay," Elizabeth replied. Then, "Why would he lie about that?'

"There's something else." Rhonda hoped Elizabeth would appreciate the implication of what she said next.

"About two weeks ago, Max stopped hitting Joey and me. I know it's ridiculous," she continued, "but I think he's planning something. I'm scared."

The open line was silent for too long.

"Elizabeth, are you there? Did you hear me?"

"Yes."

"I want to leave him. I want to take Joey and leave Max." Rhonda's tears flowed freely now.

"I'm not gloating, but I have to say, I've waited years to hear those words come out of your mouth," Elizabeth replied, calm, steady, and cautious.

"I don't know what he's planning to do, but I feel like Joey and I have to get away from him." Rhonda paused before finishing. "You were right about him. He's not a good person."

"Hah! Well, that's the understatement of the year," gloated Elizabeth. "Sorry. I'm sorry. That wasn't helpful."

"I deserved it," said Rhonda. *How had I never seen this?* "Was it always so obvious?"

"Rhonda, sweetheart, Dad was an evil man, and you married the same monster in a different skin. I guess you were just following mom's example."

The blow hurt, but Elizabeth was right.

What the hell were you thinking?

"So, you *do* think he's planning something, too?"

Elizabeth's reply was quick and blunt. "I don't just think he's planning something. I think he's already doing it."

Rhonda didn't know what that meant. She'd had her suspicions after finding the insurance policies, but how that related to Max's new *nonviolent* behavior eluded her.

"What do you think he's doing?" Rhonda whispered.

"He's letting you heal," said Elizabeth. "He doesn't want any unexplained, suspicious bruises or wounds on you or Joey that might raise questions...during an autopsy. That might cast doubt. That might keep the insurance company from paying out. That might send him to prison."

Rhonda gasped. The statement hung in the air around her like a swirling cloud of indictment. This was her fault. She'd been so trusting, so naive about Max, so stupid. But everything Elizabeth said rang true in Rhonda's mind.

"Elizabeth, what do I do?"

"Leave him, like you said. You'll all come here to Morgantown next week for Thanksgiving. And then *we'll* kick him to the curb. Believe me, I've wanted to do that for a long time."

"But I don't have a car. Well, I do, but Max keeps the keys, and he'll never agree to come to *your* house," protested Rhonda. She wanted this now more than anything. But she had no transportation, and she didn't think this was enough to go to the police. They'd laugh her out of the building for being suspicious of a husband who wasn't violent, who provided a stable, comfortable home. And now she and Joey didn't even have bruises to prove his past abuse.

What about the baby?

That was an accident!

Elizabeth was quiet for a minute, but Rhonda didn't notice. Her mind dutifully filled the dead air with her surfeit of faults.

Finally, Elizabeth spoke. "You need to convince him to drive you here. It'll be a wonderful family Thanksgiving in the country. If he's planning what I suspect, I don't think getting him to agree will take much. After all, getting you and Joey out in the country alone would be the perfect opportunity for him."

Icy water rushed over Rhonda's body; the final wretched shreds of her marital fantasy washed away. She didn't share her sister's conviction, though. She didn't think driving to the country was enough to entice Max. He hated Elizabeth, for her lesbian lifestyle, for being an academic—*a liberal*, but especially because Elizabeth never put up with his shit. They were like tigers circling each other the few times they'd been together.

"I don't know, Elizabeth."

"Tell him I'm ready to buy out your half of the house. And I want you all here to celebrate."

After the death of their parents, the house had gone to both Elizabeth and Rhonda. After the wedding, Max insisted Elizabeth buy Rhonda's half of the house since Elizabeth lived there without paying Rhonda anything. But she'd refused, for which Rhonda was secretly grateful.

A spark flared in Rhonda's head. *Yes!* she thought.

"Okay," said Rhonda. "He's always hated that you were living there *rent free.*"

"I'll email the directions. I discovered a beautiful route through the mountains while researching my last book. It's a little bumpy in places, but it'll shave a good hour off the interstate route. I think you and Joey will be safe if Max believes there's a pot of gold waiting here for him."

Could this really work? Max was obsessed with money. The thought of getting one hundred fifty thousand dollars from Elizabeth might be enough to convince him to go. *Yes,* she nodded. She was sure it would.

"Alright," said Rhonda. "And Elizabeth," her breath caught in her throat, the relief swelling her heart, "thank you."

"Oh, my sweet Rhonda, it's what sisters are for. I'll send the directions soon."

"I love you," said Rhonda.

"I love you, too, my brave little rabbit. It's time to come home."

Rhonda fed Joey his favorite frozen pizza for dinner that night. Still dressed in his school clothes: black sneakers with the swoosh on the side colored in with a pink highlighter, his favorite purple paisley button up shirt, and stone-washed jeans, Rhonda's heart melted. This was all for him, this beautiful creation she'd birthed into the world. Then she'd sent him up to his room before Max arrived home. Joey complied without complaint, happy to avoid contact with his father.

Max and Rhonda sat at the kitchen table, steaming teriyaki chicken and rice spread out between them. Max shoveled the food into his mouth. Rhonda pushed hers around the plate with her fork. Max was in a foul mood, some contentious meeting at work. But Rhonda was determined.

"Elizabeth invited us all to her house next week, for Thanksgiving," she said. She glanced up from her plate to see that Max had stopped chewing. He swallowed hard and glowered at her with dark, angry eyes.

Before he could berate Rhonda with all the reasons why he would never attend a holiday with her *fucking lesbian, liberal sister*, Rhonda found her nerve again and hurried along.

"She says she's finally ready to buy my half of the house. She thinks it's time, and she wants us all together for Thanksgiving in our childhood home to celebrate. Isn't that a lovely idea?"

Max's expression morphed so rapidly that it took Rhonda's breath away.

"Well," he said, lowering his fork. A magnanimous grin spread across his face—handsome enough for Rhonda to *almost* forget what kind of monster lurked behind those dark, sparkling eyes— "It's about fucking time."

His transformation was astonishing. Rhonda couldn't believe her eyes, or her ears. "So, it's okay? We can all go?"

"Consider it my gift. It'll be a Thanksgiving to remember, I'm sure," replied Max. Then he stabbed a hunk of chicken on his plate and crammed it into his mouth, chewing it with savage vigor.

Chapter 3

Joey sloshed in the bath, sending sudsy waves precariously close to the rim of the tub.

"Whoops," he giggled. He'd be fourteen in a few weeks but still preferred a bath to taking a shower. Soaking in a warm tub soothed his mind and body. It was his safe place from his father, who never ventured in here.

He couldn't believe his father actually agreed to the trip to Elizabeth's for Thanksgiving. It was almost the best early birthday present he could've wished for. The *best* thing would have been kissing Dennis from school. A sly grin eased across his lips. Did Dennis feel the same way? He wasn't sure. Which meant it wasn't going to happen, yet. Joey had learned one lesson well from his father—never let your guard down. He was afraid making the first move might ruin his friendship with Dennis. That was something he wasn't willing to risk.

Maybe by Christmas.

That made him smile and stirred him *down there*, exhilarating and terrifying all at the same time.

His excitement settled, and Joey dipped his chin below the waterline. Thoughts of his father bled his mood to a stark, choking dread.

Running his hands over his submerged body—the new growth of hair still fascinated him—Joey noted the tenderness on his left side, just below his ribs, was gone. The bruises had faded. It had been almost three weeks since the last time his father hit him. He was grateful, but he distrusted the respite. His father was up to something. The simmering hate never left his eyes.

Joey would rather it was just him and his mom going to Elizabeth's, but his father insisted the whole family go, which was weird. His father hated Elizabeth. Joey assumed it was because she was a lesbian. His father loathed *queers*. But to Joey, his aunt Elizabeth's company was a safe harbor from his father's storm. He never hit Joey or his mother when she came to visit. *And we're going to be there for a whole week!* He'd never been to West Virginia before, at least not that he could remember. He knew Elizabeth lived in the same house she and his mom grew up in.

His mom had been packing like they were evacuating from a hurricane since before Joey woke up that morning. Joey had finished his packing, and his suitcase sat perched at the foot of his bed in his adjoining bedroom. But he needed his bath time. They would be stuck for hours in the car with his father. The warm bath water calmed his nerves.

A thump sounded from his bedroom beyond the closed door. Joey half heard it. He was deep in thought about Elizabeth's house and lingering contemplations of Dennis. The alarm bells in his head were slow to sound, until he remembered the pictures.

Oh crap!

Joey bolted upright in the tub. Water dribbled over the edge and onto the tile floor. Footsteps thudded across the adjoining bedroom. The bathroom door flew open and banged against the wall. His father towered in the doorway, his furious eyes locked on Joey, crouching in the tub, covering his privates with trembling hands.

"You fucking little faggot!" He charged into the room, slamming the door shut behind him. He flung the shredded men's underwear ads in Joey's face.

Joey had left them on his bed, intending to hide them back under his mattress. His mind flashed to him setting them down. Then he'd forgotten all about them, the bathtub calling.

Adrenalin surged, but his legs turned to jelly. He flopped back down in the tub with a thump. Water splashed up over the rim. Joey wiped the bits of torn photos from where they'd stuck to his wet body. The shreds of paper slowly sank into the tub in a swirling dark cloud of inky water. Joey stared at his father in mortified terror.

His heart pounded against his ribs; his entire body trembled. Joey was no match for his father's brute strength. He was a growing teenager, but slight of build like his mother, and he stood zero chance against his father's powerful violence.

"You think I'm going to allow a little fucking queer to live under my roof?" His father's voice was seething, spittle flew from his lips, his face beet-red. His eyes flashed a dark menace that ripped out Joey's heart.

A violent shiver raced through him as Joey sat with his hands clutched at his chest. "Dad, I'm sorry!"

"Fuck your, *sorry!*"

His father lunged forward. His powerful hands gripped Joey's shoulders and forced him down with the might of a freight train. Driven down onto his back in the tub, Joey's legs kicked up out of the water, and his head plunged below the surface.

Oh fuck!

The pulsing underwater acoustics throbbed in Joey's ears as he lashed out and tried to free himself from his father's iron grip. He could hear the muffled bass of his father's voice, the words smothered blobs of sound. The soapy water stung his eyes. His heart slammed in his chest. His lungs screamed for air.

Joey was about to succumb to his searing desperation for air and take a breath of dirty bath water. Then the pressure on his shoulders vanished, and his father jerked him up under the arms and brought his head above the water.

Joey gasped and drew in a deep, ragged breath. His lungs spasmed in relief. Then he moaned, bent over the tub's rim, and vomited onto the soaked bathmat.

"You disgust me. Clean up this mess and get your faggot ass downstairs." His father glared at Joey, then opened the door and stormed out.

Tears fell from Joey's eyes as he stared at his sick on the floor. A terrible growing ache pounded in his head.

I guess he's done being nice.

Joey knew he should have told someone about his father. His mother knew all about it, but she was stuck with him—and she hadn't told anyone either. Fear squeezed Joey's chest in a vise. His father was handsome, successful, educated, and an accomplished actor. No one was going to believe a *little queer* like Joey.

He wouldn't be old enough to leave home for another four years. *Might as well be forever.* He didn't know how to endure it, but he had no choice. His father's anger hadn't subsided after all, but at least he hadn't hit Joey. That was something, right?

From the open doorway, his father's voice bellowed from the front hall downstairs.

"Is all of this luggage necessary? We're only going for a week!"

"Leave it there," his father said, as Joey lugged his suitcase out to the car in the driveway. His father stood by the open trunk, cleaning under his fingernails with his pocketknife. He scowled at Joey.

"Any more of your faggot filth in there?" He gestured toward Joey's luggage with the point of the knife blade.

Joey couldn't meet his father's dark, intense stare. He shivered in the cold morning breeze.

"No, sir." Joey set the suitcase down behind the car. All he'd packed were a Stephen King book, his toothbrush, and a week's worth of clothes.

His mom dragged the last suitcase out the front door, its wheels squealing under the weight. Joey glanced up and caught the sidelong look of contempt from his father.

I despise you, both.

A frigid, brittle fear shot down Joey's spine, like ice about to shatter from a hammer blow.

Joey listened to his mother's high-pitched laughter echoing back from the front seat of the car as they drove west. Not her normal, throaty guffaw. Though there'd been precious few times when his mother laughed out loud, what Joey heard now sounded forced and nervous to his ears.

"Oh, Max, that's silly!" said Rhonda. "How could anyone mistake a crow for a blue jay?"

"Doesn't matter," insisted Max, eyes on the road. "The point is no one even saw it stealing the damn fries!" He erupted in riotous laughter.

Rhonda giggled, then sighed, as though running out of steam.

To Joey, the nonsensical banter was a fraud. Its cadence stilted. *Who are these people? What the heck is going on?* And just like that, he understood. It was all fluff. His mother was in a near-manic state, and his father *never* laughed. Joey realized they were just filling empty air, pretending things were fine. Pretending they were a happy little family, going on a happy little trip.

What the frack? This is so messed up.

Cresting the spine of the Appalachians, they crossed into West Virginia. Studying the mountainous landscape capped by a slat gray sky, Joey's stomach clenched as a light but steady snow began to fall.

Chapter 4

Rhonda studied the page of directions. Elizabeth knew her stuff. She'd meticulously drawn out a map and written simple, point-by-point directions to get them to Morgantown. The alternate route, where they'd leave the main roads, would cut nearly an hour from their travel time. That information alone had won Max's endorsement.

Locals called the area the Hollows, one hundred square miles of jumbled, twisting mountains and deep serpentine valleys. There were no towns and only a few old homesteads—all abandoned. The name seemed familiar to Rhonda, but she couldn't say why. She'd never been here before. Elizabeth cautioned them to fill the gas tank before starting that leg of the trip. They stopped for a break in the quaint town of Monroy, West Virginia. Now they turned off the state highway onto the first narrow, unmarked road. The dense, leafless forest swallowed them.

Rhonda studied the map. There were eight turns in all. She didn't want to make any mistakes out here in the middle of nowhere. Apprehension crept over her as claustrophobia thudded in her head and tightened her chest. The steep mountains closed in around them as the narrow, pitted road—its edges frayed from worn, pockmarked asphalt to dirt—snaked its way deeper into the desolate landscape. Tangles of heavy timber and scrub brush clung to the steep mountainsides. Rhonda watched nervously as snow accumulated lightly on the trees and road.

Max handled the car well, having been raised in upstate New York. The light coating covering the road seemed of little concern to him. What challenged his skills were the nearly constant sharp curves and shifting grades of the road. In a few spots, the road narrowed to a single lane, jagged rock only a few feet from either side of the car.

"How far to the next turn?" asked Max, his voice flat, eyes riveted to the road.

"There should be a turn about half a mile ahead. She's listed it as a trail," Rhonda said. "We don't turn there; it's just a marker. One mile past the trail, we make a right onto the next road." With something to focus on, Rhonda felt her jitters calm. She kept her eyes peeled for the trail.

Joey sat quietly in the back seat. The scenery was interesting, very rugged, probably the wildest landscape he'd ever seen up close. He still had the headache that came on rapidly after he threw up earlier, but he'd had worse. He shifted in his seat and his foot slipped, inadvertently kicking the underside of his father's seat.

"What the fuck are you doing?!" His father shot a look at Joey in the rearview mirror.

"I'm sorry, dad! I'm sorry!" The last thing Joey wanted was to cause a crash.

"Just fucking sit there! Don't fucking move."

Joey felt like he was barreling toward his doom and had no way to stop it.

An icy hand gripped Rhonda's gut. Max's easygoing demeanor had vanished. She wasn't sure why Elizabeth would send them along this route. Rhonda didn't care how much time it would save. She would have happily sat in the car for that extra hour to avoid this growing anxiety. But for some reason, Max had jumped at the alternate route. Thrilled at the prospect of spending less time in the car, she assumed.

"I think that's the trail," she said quickly, as they shot by a deep hollow on their left.

"I saw it." Max glanced at the odometer.

Chapter 5

Joey's head swooned in nauseating swirls, like he'd stood up too quickly. Their car lurched as his father struggled for control. Then the vertigo retreated as fast as it came. The road, which had narrowed with every mile, was now a rutted two-track.

"Oh my God. What's happened?" Rhonda frantically scanned the swirling world outside the windshield.

Joey felt a suffocating blanket of anxiety envelope him. Its tight heavy weave squeezed the breath out of him. Billowing curtains of snow obscured their way. Half a foot of snow coated the road, like it had oozed up from the ground.

This is wrong. This can't possibly be the right way. Joey wanted to scream. His hand seized the armrest on the door in a vise-like grip.

"Watch out!" screamed Rhonda. Her hands shot up to brace against the dashboard.

Max slammed on the brakes. The car skidded to a stop at the bottom of a hill. The road had dead-ended, blocked by impenetrable forest. He tried reverse and was rewarded with the shriek of tires spinning on ice. The forest faded into gloom and night approached like a menacing stranger.

Max had recently purchased the car, but he'd skimped on features. There was only rear wheel drive. And there was no satellite emergency service system.

Max slammed his fists against the steering wheel.

"Goddamn it!" He swiveled toward Rhonda, spittle flying from his mouth as he screamed, "How fucking hard can it be to follow a set of directions!"

Rhonda shrank against the passenger door.

"I'm so sorry, Max! This makes no sense!"

She held up the sheet of directions like a shield. She glanced in bewilderment at the worthless paper in her hands, then at her husband panting in frustrated rage behind the wheel.

"We followed the directions exactly as Elizabeth wrote them."

She stared at the paper, horrified by its betrayal.

Joey sat stunned, his heart galloping in his chest.

This can't be happening.

He'd known plenty of fear, but his breath surrendered to this new terror coursing through him. His father's punches couldn't hold a candle to it. He felt sure he was going to vomit again. He retreated into himself, knowing from experience not to say anything. *Keep quiet. Don't get on his radar.* Joey scrunched himself against the rear door behind his father's seat. His heart drummed double-time in his narrow chest, as his father raged.

Max pummeled the steering wheel with his fists. Then he lashed out and slapped Rhonda hard across the face, sharp and clear as a firecracker. Joey gasped. His mother screamed in pain and dropped the directions as her hands flew up to protect her face.

Joey froze. His wild eyes stared at his parents in numbed panic. His father drew back like he was going to strike out again, but instead he released his seat belt and threw open his door.

"Get out!" he yelled, as he climbed out of the car.

Rhonda scrambled to release her seat belt and comply with her husband's command.

Joey couldn't move. He didn't want to get out of the car. He envisioned his father jumping back in and locking Joey and his mother out in the cold. He knew his father wouldn't abandon them, only because he couldn't. The car was stuck. But he could leave them outside to freeze to death.

Is this it? Is this where he finally goes berserk?

Joey's heart palpitated. He fought back another wave of nausea as he realized this was the moment he'd always most dreaded.

Rhonda opened her door. Joey still hadn't moved. Max yanked open the rear door and glared at his son.

"I said, get out!"

Joey fumbled to release his seat belt. He scrambled out of the car under his father's seething stare. Falling snow instantly coated him.

"Push the snow away from the tires. Make a clear track, so I can back up." Max's anger had deflated; his voice now tinged with a nervous edge.

Two attempts to free the car failed. The tires could gain no traction on the sloped road. The snow continued piling up. They weren't going anywhere.

The sharp, sour scent of sweat and fear swamped them as they climbed back into the car. Max glared out the windshield. Rhonda huddled against the passenger-side door casting furtive glances at her husband. Joey tried to slow his breathing, closing his eyes as the sting of exhaustion and fear overloaded his mind.

Just breathe. Just breathe. Just breathe.

Joey opened his eyes. He stared at the snow and darkness. His heart plummeted with the realization that they were stranded in the middle of the wilderness. He shivered even as the car's heater blasted out balmy air. And to make matters worse, he felt a sharp, surging pressure in his bladder. He hadn't used the restroom at the gas station in Monroy.

This just gets worse and worse.

His mother stared blankly out at the snow falling through the beams of the headlights like New Year's confetti. She absently rubbed her cheek and cast a brief flash of wounded betrayal at Joey's father. Her hands were shaking.

His parents checked for a signal on their phones, but there were zero bars in the depths of the Hollows.

Joey couldn't hold back any longer.

"Mom, I need to go to the bathroom." His eyes were downcast in shame.

"Well, of course you do." His father turned and glared over his shoulder at Joey. "Why the fuck didn't you go at the gas station?"

Joey had nothing to say, but he knew he had to answer.

"I didn't have to go then." He stared at his fidgeting hands in his lap.

"Typical," his father said, but he'd lost interest.

"Go on." His mother glanced at his father, then out at the dizzying snow. "But hurry, sweetheart."

"Okay, Mom."

Joey opened his door and stepped out of the car. He plunged mid-shins into snow.

Oh my God, we're never getting out of here.

His father growled at his mother as Joey closed the door, but Joey heard him just fine. "You coddle him all the fucking time. That's why he's a goddamn faggot. You know that, right? It's your fault."

Joey winced in anticipation of another smack, but it didn't come. His father sat brooding as the last of the day's dreary light faded completely.

Joey's feet crunched through the snow, slipping several times as he climbed the short, rocky bank next to the road. At the top, he stepped a few feet into the trees to get out of sight of the car and his parents. The sun was gone. The only illumination were the headlights reflecting off the snow. Deep shadows crowded in. His teeth chattered.

His bladder felt ready to burst and steam rose as his stream surged out like a geyser. He sighed into the freezing air, his breath a fog enveloping his head. Snow accumulated on his shoulders as a thin smile of relief crawled across his lips.

Beyond the thick wall of saplings in front of the car—bright and stark in the headlight's glare—the forest stood inky black. He caught a glimpse of something. His heart jackhammered.

There's a light!

Chapter 6

Max's eyes darted absently as his mind rushed to revise his plan. His only real problem was how *he* would get out of there. He wasn't stupid, and he was great at math. And it hadn't taken much to add up the extra luggage Rhonda had packed, with Elizabeth's sudden change of heart about buying the house and wanting them to come for Thanksgiving. Rhonda thought she had pulled a fast one on him. She thought she was so smart—smarter than him. She thought she'd found a way to leave him. But what she'd done was dig her own fucking grave, and one for Joey, too. There was never going to be any money from Elizabeth. But there was sure as hell going to be a payday from the insurance company if he played his cards right.

It would be a simple thing to dispose of Rhonda and Joey. The perfect situation had been thrown into his lap. People died of exposure in the woods all the time. He could help them along by breaking an arm or leg, or two. Maybe he could lock them out until they froze, and then load them back into the car, as though they'd died waiting while he went for help.

That still left him with a stuck car and fifteen miles back to the state road. Could he walk all that way in the snow? He had his doubts. He was healthy and strong and thought it possible, but it would be an arduous hike. It would make a convincing cover, though—if he made it. He could see the headline now.

Man walks fifteen miles in brutal snowstorm to summon help for his stranded family, who tragically perished in his absence.

He liked the sound of that.

He would finally be rid of his biggest mistake. Excitement swelled his chest like a balloon of possibilities. And the cherry on top, was the insurance he'd taken out on all three of them—it wouldn't have looked right to insure his family and not himself. Any loving husband and father would want to be sure his family was financially secure in the event of his own death. That was just common sense. That's how much he cared. And he hadn't taken out the policies recently, like an amateur. He'd done that over a year and a half ago. That's when he'd finally decided to emancipate himself.

That's how you don't get caught.

The only thing that niggled at his mind was, why did Elizabeth send them out here to the middle of nowhere? It was like she was trying to get rid of them. He'd seen the directions, and for all his bluster, he knew Rhonda had followed them exactly. So, what was the deal? Why would Elizabeth set him up with the perfect opportunity to kill his family and get away with it?

His thoughts jolted as Joey yanked open the rear door and clambered back inside the car, stumbling excitedly over his words.

"There's a house or cabin or something, through the trees! I saw a light!"

Fuck.

"Where did you see it?" Joey's claim had unbalanced Max. He had to admit that a quick bolt of relief had shot through him, but it couldn't dispel the annoyance this new element presented to his plan. With a push of a button, the car's dome light glared down. Max's eyes twinkled as Joey winced at the brightness.

Joey pointed excitedly toward the windshield.

"That way," he said. "Through the trees." His face was flushed from the cold, but his eyes glistened with relief.

"How far?" asked Rhonda, her eyes flashing expectantly from Max to her son, hands fidgeting in her lap, desperate, pathetic hope brimming on her face.

Joey looked down for a moment, then back to his mother, but he avoided looking at Max.

"I couldn't tell." Then his face lit up. "But it looked like fire, like a candle or lantern or something. It was flickering. I wouldn't have been able to see it if it was too far away."

"We have to go see," implored Rhonda.

Max still wasn't convinced.

"We have to. We can't just sit here. We're getting buried in snow."

"Maybe there's another road over there," said Joey. "Maybe there's a house, people, a phone."

Max was loath to admit it, but they were right. They couldn't just sit here. And where there was a house, there might be someone lurking around. Maybe he wasn't as free as he'd thought he was, to deal with his family as he pleased.

"Max?"

He grimaced at the high, whiny note of expectation in Rhonda's voice. But he relented.

"Fine. Let's go see."

Chapter 7

Elizabeth guided her vintage four-wheel-drive Bronco cautiously down the gloomy interstate, as light snow continued to fall. The radio had initially forecast a couple of inches, but now two weather systems would join to form a nor'easter. Significant accumulation was possible. But the worst of the snow wasn't expected until late tomorrow night, giving her plenty of time.

Rhonda had always been too trusting, always ready to give the benefit of the doubt, forgive and forget, setting her own self-interests aside. Elizabeth scowled and gritted her teeth in frustration. But she consoled herself that Rhonda had finally come to her senses. *And it couldn't have come at a better time.* Her face bloomed in a smile.

She'd detested Max from the first. He was brutish with a deep malevolence in his eyes—a lifeless, uncaring darkness, like a gun ready to fire.

The malevolence he harbored frightened her. Always ready to threaten or pounce. She'd tried to convince Rhonda that he was *not* the one for her. But Rhonda had been captivated by him.

Reluctantly Elizabeth admitted Max was physically beautiful to a cliché—if you liked that sort of thing—tall, muscular, darkly tanned, and handsome. He was a striking man at first glance. And Elizabeth knew Rhonda's low self-esteem, an issue since her earliest childhood, had blinded her to the danger Max presented. She couldn't see that she deserved better.

When Rhonda had confided that Max sometimes got a little too angry and slapped her, Elizabeth's worst fears were realized. Rhonda downplayed it and suggested that it was really her fault. She just did stupid things that set Max off. *Silly me,* she'd say.

Elizabeth suspected it had started in the early days, but it wasn't until a few years after Joey was born that Rhonda told her about it.

Elizabeth couldn't bring herself to contemplate what had *really* happened to the baby. Rhonda had given Elizabeth the same story she'd told the doctors. *I tripped and fell down the stairs.*

But in the last year, it had become so much worse. No one was that accident-prone. Always, Rhonda took the blame. *I'm such a klutz. Silly me.* She refused to call the police—even going as far as forbidding Elizabeth to do so with the threat of never speaking to her again, of telling the police that she, Elizabeth, was making it all up.

But when Rhonda called her about the insurance policies, Elizabeth knew time was up. She'd always suspected what Max was capable of, and now she knew she'd been right. The relief had been like a mountain lifted from her heart when Rhonda said she was ready to leave Max.

FINALLY!

Elizabeth had a plan—a way to stop Max before he could do what she was positive he planned to do; murder her sister and nephew. She just needed a little help. And she'd known just who to ask. She didn't believe for a moment that Max would just let Rhonda and Joey walk away.

It was dark now. She signaled her exit from the interstate. There were no other cars on the road, only the falling snow. She slowed the Bronco gently, to avoid skidding at the bottom of the exit ramp. The road showed no tire tracks marring the fresh snow on its surface, just an unbroken ribbon of white stretching into the darkened landscape. She turned left and headed toward Monroy.

Chapter 8

Miss Gortham yawned, covering her mouth with a wrinkled hand, and reminded herself that she was just getting started tonight. She was settled in her worn, but comfortable, wingback chair in the cozy living room of her beloved cottage. The cottage had been her great grandfather's. Her mother, and Miss Gortham herself, had both grown up here. Now it was hers. She'd lived there alone since her younger sister married and moved out forty years ago.

Glancing at her grandmother's ticking pendulum clock hanging on the wall, she saw that the time had arrived.

All these years, and now it seemed the family debt would finally be paid. "What a wonderful thing," she said.

For the first time, she allowed herself a moment of excitement before tamping it down. It was too soon for that. She had hope, but she'd had hope before. She knew that was a trail leading to heartbreak if she let it take hold too strongly at this early stage. Still...

She stood and felt a new burst of energy surge through her seventy-five-year-old body. She walked with her usual measured cadence to the closet by the front door, retrieved her dark wool coat, and pulled it on. She'd changed from her low-heeled shoes to the new, sturdier leather walking shoes her nephew gave her. He was such a thoughtful man.

Turning to the ornate glass-paneled front door, she stared through the panes of rippled, etched glass, waiting. Her heart fluttered in her chest with an excitement years in the making.

Minutes later, headlights rounded the bend in the road that passed her house. The black Bronco pulled into the driveway, drove up the hill, and stopped behind Miss Gortham's own small car. Then it flashed its high beams like something out of a John le Carré spy novel, and Miss Gortham stepped out into the night.

Chapter 9

"She told me she's been through here dozens of times," said Rhonda, repeating Elizabeth's words. "She said, 'It's perfectly safe.'"

Max had retrieved their heavier footwear from the trunk, along with Rhonda's winter coat. Max and Joey were already wearing theirs. He'd also taken the flashlight from the emergency kit.

Suited up to the best of their ability, Max turned off the car's engine and killed the lights, plunging them into perfect darkness. Their eyes had yet to adjust to the ambient light of a full moon above the storm clouds.

The moment jarred into pandemonium when Max switched on the flashlight. Its bright beam speared the darkness, jagged light in chaotic motion as he juggled the flashlight while jamming the key fob into his coat pocket.

Joey waited in the back seat as his parents got ready. Trying to steady his shaking hands, his heart thudded heavily in his chest. He was sure he'd seen the light through the trees, but now he was second-guessing the memory.

He struggled to push away the doubt. If he was wrong, they were truly screwed, and he knew it.

They were miles from anywhere, heavy snow was falling—the heaviest he had ever seen—and their car was stuck. Visions of their frozen bodies filled his mind, buried in the snow until spring. Found at last by some hapless traveler who'd had the common sense to wait for warmer weather before exploring this forgotten part of the state. It took a moment for his father's brusque voice to filter through his thoughts.

"Joey! Are you deaf?"

Joey snapped out of it. "I'm ready," he said.

"Show us where you saw the light."

They opened the car doors, pushing back the accumulated snow. Swirling torrents of snow streamed in as they climbed out. With the engine turned off, the soft susurrus of falling snow met their ears, as gentle as falling feathers.

"Oh!" exclaimed Rhonda. As she stepped into the snow, the tops of her shoes sank well below the surface of the deep powder. She recoiled from the cold like a fresh slap to her face.

Max swung the flashlight beam into Joey's eyes.

"Which way?"

Wincing, Joey ducked his head and raised a hand to block the stabbing beam of light from his eyes. He pointed with his other hand, as he had a few minutes before. His father knew which way—he was just being a prick.

Max grunted and turned the light toward the trees. He moved forward without waiting for Joey or his mother, and without making any effort to illuminate their path. He trudged along, crunching through the snow. The flashlight beam darted in frantic motion as he slipped here and there and flailed his arms for balance.

Joey rounded the back of the car and steadied his mother, helping her forward with a hand on her elbow and an arm around her waist. Stepping unsteadily on the slippery ground, she soon found her equilibrium. She patted Joey's arm in thanks, and he withdrew a few steps behind her. The snow crunched under their feet with every step.

Max wasn't far ahead. He'd paused at the edge of the trees. He turned the flashlight down, casting a bright halo of light at his feet. He stared into the trees, leaning this way and that, trying to catch sight of the light Joey claimed to have seen.

Joey and his mother drew up beside his father, and they searched between the trees for a glimpse of the light. Joey realized the problem. Earlier, he'd been standing up on the bank above the road. They were several feet lower here. The forest ahead of them was dark and still. There was a tangle of young saplings, a few still carrying the withered leaves of fall, creating a virtual wall between the road and the forest beyond. There was a gap off to the left and Joey stepped toward it.

"Dad, shine the light over here," Joey said.

His father didn't reply, but he moved the beam of light to where Joey was walking.

Pushing the smaller saplings aside, Joey stepped through the widened gap.

"Looks like a trail," Joey said, over his shoulder. He could see a short distance into the woods. The flashlight beam filtered through the tangle of saplings, casting fingers of light deeper into the forest. A path wound its way into the depths of the dark. As he moved a few steps forward, gaining some elevation, he peered around the massive oak in front of him. The flickering light flashed again, far ahead. Its shimmering glow seemed to float in the solid mass of the black night. The path appeared to wind in the direction of the light.

"I see it!" called Joey. A rush of excitement and relief washed over him.

"Oh, thank God," sighed his mother.

Joey waited for his parents to join him on the trail. He turned back from their approaching forms to the light in the woods, reassuring himself that it hadn't disappeared.

The snow pelted them heavier now. As his parents joined Joey on the trail, he moved forward a few steps so they could see.

"Huh," grunted his father.

"Oh!" squealed his mother, "I see it!"

His father turned the light on his mother. "We *all* see it."

The snow became a deluge. The light disappeared. The gentle whisper of precipitation became a raging torrent. For a few moments, there was nothing but walls of falling snow imprisoning them. His father turned the flashlight back the way they'd come, but even the car behind them was lost.

"It's getting worse," said Joey.

"It's that way," said his father, sounding less certain than his sudden, purposeful movement forward implied.

His father took the lead, tramping a path through the snow that was now a foot deep, and continuing to fall at an alarming rate. His mother followed close behind, with Joey bringing up the rear.

The dark closed in, isolating each of them. It sucked the hope from Rhonda, as the cold stole her breath. She glanced forward at the bobbing light that was Max, as he led the way through the forest.

She'd felt a spark of hope earlier when they'd finally gotten on the road, headed toward a fresh start for her and Joey. *My God*, she thought, was that really today? It seemed a million years ago.

Icy fingers caressed her heart. She no longer held any doubt about Max's intentions. His laughing and joking in the car were an act. She'd seen through it instantly. But she'd played along, because, what the hell else was she going to do?

Reaching down, Rhonda absently held her belly with both hands, and a shudder nearly toppled her from her unsteady feet.

My Baby.

She refused the thought, the snippet of memory severed.

All that pain and suffering and now they were stranded in the mountains in a severe snowstorm, and it was Max she was counting on to keep them safe. How laughable was that? She couldn't believe Elizabeth could make such a terrible mistake with the directions. Anger flared at her sister, anger that couldn't come close to covering the fresh guilt she felt for her years of submission to a murderous bully. But it quickly subsided as she wondered if she'd simply missed something in the directions, and their current plight really was all her fault, as Max had intimated.

Whoever was to blame seemed irrelevant now. They were just three lost souls wandering in the dark, snowy woods. The frigid air and accumulating snow were slowly sapping the heat and energy from her body.

They made slow progress, but the path was visible in the flashlight beam as they pushed forward. After three-quarters of an hour, with the mysterious flickering light fading and reappearing as they made their way through the trees, a log cabin finally came into view.

As the trees around them began to thin out, Rhonda thought she heard someone calling from the forest behind them. She turned and scanned the snowy, dark woods. But she saw no one, and she heard nothing more. She turned and continued the struggle forward with her husband and son.

Part Two

Worthy

Chapter 10

Ida Wheeling had startled awake in the dim, early hours of the morning. Cold and confused at the knowledge surfacing in her fuzzy mind, she'd felt a tendril of dread work up her spine like a hairy spider crawling on her skin.

How many times? She shook her head, trying her damnedest to clear the fog of sleep. She couldn't remember. Eleven or twelve, maybe?

"I ought to mark a tally on the wall or somethin'."

She lay in her parent's old bed in the corner of the cabin, her mother's colorful hand-stitched quilt spread across her like autumn leaves. Staring across the cabin that her father had built with his own two hands—the place she had lived for all her forty-nine years—the voices of her childhood echoed in her mind. Laughter and love, and hardship too, had been lived here. Her mother's loving caress, her father's gentle smile, and her brother's silly antics all brought her heart near to bursting. They were all gone now, and nothing could be done about that. The shadow of her sister's betrayal swept through her mind like filthy black bog water submerging her soul. She forced the thoughts from her mind, unable to bear them any longer.

"No matter," she'd said, her voice a croak of disuse. "Just get on with it." There was an enormous amount of work to do.

The roaring fire snapped and popped like popcorn and firecrackers in the stone fireplace. Ida added another log, tapping the end against the burning wood on the iron grate, breaking up the coals and sending sparks scurrying up the chimney. Then she laid the new log on top of the inferno. She peered into the fire, her leathery face—creased and toughened from years of sun, wind, and exhausting work—softened in the firelight.

She'd lit several tallow lamps, and the golden-yellow light cast a gentle, warm glow throughout the cabin's first-floor room. She peered up at the dark hatchway at the top of the steep stairs in the back corner of the cabin. It stood open, a maw of heavy shadow the light from below was powerless to banish.

Wearing her worn dungarees over a thick white cotton shirt, Ida carried an unlit lamp to the fireplace, clomping along in her old leather boots. Taking a thin, splintery stick from the woodpile, she lit the end in the fire and touched the sputtering flame to the thick cotton wick of the last lamp. Light flared as the wick caught the flame.

Holding back her coarse shoulder-length hair the silvery color of weathered straw, she blew out the flaming stick and set it on a tin plate on the mantel. Fitting the glass chimney back onto the lamp, she adjusted the wick until the flame glowed bright and steady.

Shuffling to the stairs, Ida climbed up to the attic. The darkness grudgingly retreated from the halo of light and was vanquished entirely as she reached the top of the stairs. She stooped slightly because the angle of the roof was low there.

Shivering, she stood upright, the steeply pitched rafters easily clearing her head as she moved away from the stairs. She could see her breath in the chilled air.

"It'll warm up soon enough."

Dust lay in a thin coating across the floor, but there was nothing to do about that. She was pressed for time. Her memory echoed the phantom sounds of her childhood, still fresh in the cold air after all these years. Nostalgia lured a fragile smile across her lips. It was always cold up here in the winter, and sweltering in the summer, yet she had nothing but fond memories of the attic. She'd always felt safe up here. That's what she remembered most of all.

Three beds of peeled log frames and sturdy ropes stretched between them in a grid pattern occupied the room. A thin mattress of burlap stuffed with straw, and a thick blanket and a pillow lay atop each one. One bed sat kitty-corner across from the stairs, where her brother, Daniel, slept as a child. A small window was set in the center of the short knee wall between Daniel's bed and her sister Eugenia's bed tucked into the other corner along that front wall, foot to foot with the window between them.

Under the window was an empty bookcase. Ida pondered where the books and knickknacks once stored there had gone. She couldn't remember. A small nightstand separated Eugenia's bed from Ida's old bed. She was the oldest and so took the honor spot closest to the stairs, which also had the most headroom, being under the ridge of the roof. Next to her bed was a pathway of a few feet in width. In the corner past the stairs stood a long set of shelves of rough-cut boards where they'd kept their clothes as children. Now they held only dust.

Although it was the same size as the cabin below, the space felt cramped in comparison. The steep roof, rising from the four-foot knee walls at the front and back of the cabin up to the ridge beam, had felt like a cathedral when she was a child.

Sighing, remembering what was coming, she carried the lamp over to the bookcase under the window and set it there. Its light shone out into the gloom of the snowy afternoon.

Alone now, her siblings long since dead—though she supposed their descendants might be out in the world somewhere—Ida turned away from the room. To keep her balance as she descended, her hand glided lightly along the hinged wooden hatch-cover leaning against the knee wall at the top of the stairs. The cover was to seal off the attic when it wasn't in use. It helped to keep the downstairs cooler in summer and warmer in winter, but she left it open now. She'd be using the space soon enough.

Ida had finished her outside chores before the snow started, feeding the chickens and shooing them back into the coop near the barn. She'd pitched hay into the stalls occupied by her cow, Sugar, who eyed her gratefully, and her old horse, Oats, who stood casually watching her. She lugged several pails of ice-cold water from the creek behind the barn and filled Sugar and Oats' water trough set into the divider between the stalls. Afterward, she'd sat on the overturned bucket for a brief rest, her breath puffing out in a gentle fog. Then she'd milked Sugar.

She'd stacked several days' worth of firewood on the front porch of the cabin—carried from the old three-sided shed tucked up against the trees out near the lane. Its tired frame leaned against the tree trunks for support, an attribute she related to.

Long shadows grew in the forest, dark fingers draining the color from the world as the last of the daylight faded. The snow began falling in earnest then. Great swirling waves of white swamped the cabin's glowing windows. Ida built up the dying fire in the wood-fired cook-stove.

Earlier, she'd gathered ingredients from the various storage bins in the kitchen and from the springhouse out by the creek. She set about making her stew for supper and left it to simmer. The blended aromas of sage, the sharp smell of dried ramps, and stewing venison filled the cabin. Her mouth watered as her stomach let out a thunderous grumble.

"Soon enough," she mumbled. She retrieved the covered loaf pans she'd set near the fireplace before stacking the firewood. Gently lifting the hand-woven dishtowels from the pans, she set them on the counter. Nodding her approval at the high rise of the pale, puffy bread dough, she breathed deeply of the tangy, yeasty scent rising up. She did love a good sourdough.

"Oh! That's gonna be good," she said. Using one of the dishtowels, she pulled open the oven door, carefully placed the bread pans inside, and quickly closed it again.

At last, she was done. Gathering up her cob pipe and pouch of tobacco from a tray on the mantel, she carefully measured out a pinch and tamped the dried leaf-crumble into the pipe's blackened bowl. The strong bittersweet aroma of tobacco blended with the acrid scent of wood smoke from the fireplace and again drew out memories. Back then, it was her father who sat and smoked this same pipe in the evening after an exhausting day's work, same as she did now.

With the stick from the mantel, she lit the pipe. Sucking on the stem, she watched the flame bobbing down into the bowl. Exhaling a mouthful of bluish-gray smoke, she blew out the stick in a puff of cloudy breath and replaced it on the tray on the mantel. Settling into one of the stuffed chairs and puffing on her pipe, Ida gazed deeply into the crackling flames in the fireplace. Like shifting fog, the pipe smoke drifted in a lazy haze, then caught on a draft and streamed toward the fireplace and up the chimney. For a few moments, she was lost in the lightheadedness from the nicotine. Then she smiled.

Chapter 11

Rhonda felt dizzy from exertion. The cold took deep bites at her face. She felt the tickle of threat on the back of her neck—a feather of warning against her skin—as though they were no longer alone. She looked to her right, straining to see anything beyond the faint outline of trees. She saw nothing to account for the overwhelming feeling of being watched. The dense forest had given way to what might have been a lovely open valley in daylight. In the dark of the snowy evening, the feeling was more akin to a deeply shadowed arena, exposed and vulnerable on every side to whatever lurked in the dim reaches of the surrounding forest.

Rhonda struggled through the snow, trailing Max by a dozen feet. Joey followed close behind her, all of them grunting through their toil like burdened oxen. A light breeze carried a sweet hint of wood smoke as it sighed through the treetops. But behind that, something else caught Rhonda's attention. Another sound, hidden behind their own crunching footfalls. Something in the forest was stomping toward them. And unlike them, it wasn't struggling. It was approaching fast and strong.

"Something's coming!" Rhonda shrieked. She'd stopped in her tracks, her eyes glued to the shifting forest behind them.

"What?" snipped Max. He halted his struggle through the deep snow and stared back at his wife, panting heavily from the exertion of breaking trail. Sweat beaded on his face, even in the frigid air. "What the hell's wrong now?"

Joey stood next to his mother, searching the woods for whatever had captured her attention.

The cabin was now visible at the far end of the clearing, maybe a hundred yards away. The hazy shapes of what appeared to be a small barn and a chicken coop stood a couple of dozen yards behind the cabin. A zigzagging, stacked-pole fence enclosed the acre between the chicken coop and where they now stood at the edge of the forest. A garden.

Trellises covered in withered vines and tall, desiccated stalks in neat rows protruded from the snow like abandoned dreams.

The trail resembled a narrow lane between the edge of the forest and the garden fence. Running in a straight line for a hundred yards, the lane made a gentle curve to the left toward the log cabin sheltered under a steeply pitched roof heavily ladened with snow. Faint smoke, rising like departing spirits, streamed skyward from the crown of a stout stone chimney built onto the far end of the cabin. Soft, creamy light shone from the windows, casting elongated trapezoid patches onto the snow-covered ground.

But they weren't looking at the cabin now. Their attention now focused on a loud threshing noise in the forest. Something was crashing through the trees toward them.

Max and Joey heard it, too. The blood drained from their flushed faces.

"What the fuck is that?" said Max.

"Hello!" Joey called out to the cabin at the top of his lungs. "HELLO!"

"Don't," screeched Rhonda. "What are you doing?" she hissed.

"I'm calling to the cabin," he said. Joey grabbed his mother's arm and pulled her along. "Come on! Hurry up!" They managed to pass his father and struggled to break trail toward the cabin.

Max didn't need to be told twice. His flashlight had found nothing to focus on other than falling snow and shifting glimpses of the forest that stood mere feet away. But whatever was moving through the woods was approaching fast.

Joey and Rhonda were high-stepping as they raced through the snow, their voices mixed in discordant pleas as they hollered at the cabin for all they were worth. "Hello!" "Help us!" "Please!"

Max abandoned his search of the trees and raced to catch up to and then pass his wife and son.

"Dad always said, 'You don't have to be faster than the bear, just faster than your friends!'" Max panted. He shoved Rhonda as he dashed by, nearly knocking her off her feet.

"Oh!" Rhonda staggered. Her arms pin-wheeled. Joey managed to grab one flailing arm and steady her. He shot an angry look at his father's back, racing toward the cabin. With the horrible stomping rapidly gaining on them, they dashed to catch up with Max as he neared the cabin's front steps.

"Hello!" Joey called again, pushing his mother forward along the trampled path left by his father.

As Max started up the steps to the cabin, the front door flew open with a metallic shriek of hinges. The menacing silhouette of a woman appeared, backlit by the lamplight flooding out from the open doorway. A twelve-gauge shotgun was hefted to her shoulder, the barrel pointing directly at Max's chest.

"Whoa!" Max shouted. He drew up in surprise. Raising his hands defensively, he stepped backward. He missed the step and fell sideways into sixteen inches of snow with a soft thud.

The pursuing stomping grew deafening. In daylight, they'd certainly be able to see whatever caused it. It had to be gigantic. The woman raised the shotgun barrel above Joey and Rhonda's heads. Seating the butt of the gun firmly against her shoulder, she pulled the trigger.

The explosion of gunpowder nearly burst Rhonda's eardrums, the muzzle flash blinding as it flared. The woman grunted at the shock to her shoulder, but it seemed more from reflex than pain.

Rhonda screamed. She and Joey ducked.

Silence followed, save for the wind and falling snow. Whatever chased them had stopped.

"Quickly." The woman beckoned from the porch.

As Max struggled to right himself, Rhonda and Joey hurried by him and up the steps, not sparing him a single glance.

"We're lost!" Rhonda squealed, looking back over her shoulder. But there was nothing there. The shotgun blast had done its job and scared whatever it was away, or at least stayed its advance. The forest was silent save for the constant whispering of falling snow among the trees, a gossip of forest secrets only they understood.

"Please help us," implored Rhonda.

The woman looked past them, squinting into the darkness. The forest's edge was a hazy scrim against the darker depths beyond. She nodded as though coming to a decision.

"Better come in," she said, her voice rusty and gruff. She stepped back into the cabin. The shotgun rested in the crook of her arm, its deadly bore aimed at the floor.

"Thank you," gushed Rhonda. She and Joey shuffled by the woman, stamping the snow from their boots before entering her home. Max brushed the caked snow off himself. He glanced back to the woods and quickly followed the others into the cabin.

Rhonda glanced back and caught the look of amusement cross the woman's face as Max passed by her, partially shadowed by the wide brim of her old leather hat. She followed them inside and slammed the cabin door closed.

Chapter 12

The cabin was stuffy, the air heavy with the scents of cooking food, wood smoke, and the sharp, thick smell of burned pipe tobacco. They quickly began shedding their coats as the woman set the shotgun back onto its pegs on the wall by the door. She shucked out of her sheepskin coat and hung it on a peg under the shotgun.

"What was that?" stammered Max. He struggled with his coat zipper.

"No idea. Could'a been a bear. Maybe somethin' else," said the woman.

"Do you have a phone?" asked Max, attempting to hide his recent terror. Finally free of his coat, he folded it over his arm. Joey and Rhonda stood next to Max. All eyes were on the strange woman.

She clucked lightly and said, "No," her voice softer now, but still slightly scratchy. She took off her floppy leather hat and hung it on top of her coat, her weathered-straw hair hanging to her shoulders.

"No, I don't have a phone, never have." She nodded to the hooks on the wall below the shotgun. "You can hang your coats there." The lilting twang of her words evoked the rugged mountains in which she lived.

"We were driving to my sister's house in Morgantown," explained Rhonda. "Our car got stuck, and we saw...my son Joey," Rhonda looked at Joey and put a hand on his shoulder. "Joey saw the light from your cabin." Rhonda finished as abruptly as she'd started, as though she'd run out of words.

"Morgantown's a fair piece off," said the woman. "Haven't been there since I was a girl," she said wistfully. "I 'magine it's changed a bit since then."

"Well," said Max. "We need to get our car out. Do you have any neighbors with a phone? Is there a town nearby?" His pompous tone drew a strange smile to the woman's chapped lips.

Rhonda bristled at Max's disrespectful tone and nodded apologetically at the woman who'd taken them in.

"No, no neighbors this far out." Her face brightened. "There's Monroy, the town about thirty miles from here."

Max's impatience exploded, "We know where Monroy is! We've just come from there!" He looked around the cabin, his face pinched in disgust.

The woman's face hardened. "Well," she spat. "Then I guess you know you're shit outa luck, don't cha?"

Joey laughed—the woman's words were so unexpected. He was delighted by her confidence.

"Sorry," he said, his face blooming red. He turned his eyes to the floor, but not before he spied a tiny grin twitch the corners of the woman's mouth. It shed years from her face, and he questioned why he'd thought she was old. One minute her face was wrinkled as a raisin, and the next, her skin, still leathery, glowed with a taut, youthful radiance. Throughout, her pale blue eyes sparkled with life and mystery.

"Ma'am, thank you for inviting us into your home," Rhonda said. "We sincerely appreciate it." She looked at Joey, and then Max, who appeared to be struggling to keep his anger under control. He was silent.

The woman nodded and smiled at Rhonda and Joey. Then she cast a quick scowl at Max before dismissing him from her regard.

"Honey, you're more'n welcome. Hang your coats and make yourselves to home. I was just gettin' my supper ready, and I'd be real pleased if you'd all join me."

Max looked furious but calmed by increments. Then something occurred to him.

"Is your husband here, or a son? Do you have a truck?"

The woman glanced at Max, noting the obvious contempt for her still gracing his face. "No. I live alone," she said. "Have for years. Never owned a car. I got my old horse, Oats, but he can barely pull the plow through the garden anymore. He'd be no help pulling a heavy car in the snow."

Rhonda hung her coat on a hook by the door and warmed herself by the fireplace. She gazed at the other woman in wonder.

"You live here alone?" Rhonda looked incredulous. "How do you manage? How do you get supplies?" The thought of it seemed to frighten her. Her eyes were wide with horror or admiration. Joey couldn't tell which.

"Oh honey, the land provides most of what I need to get by." She paused, another knowing smile creasing her weathered face. "And people sometimes bring me things."

"Well, that's all very nice for you," said Max. Then, he composed himself and continued more calmly. "When might you be expecting any of these people next? Won't someone be coming to check on you with this storm?"

It seemed a reasonable question, but the woman just shook her head gently. "No, no one else is coming." She thought for a moment, and then asked, "Could you tell me what the date is?" It was the most vulnerable she'd looked thus far. Her face turned to them expectantly, like a lost child.

It was a puzzling question, but of course, a woman living out in the woods by herself would likely lose track of the days easily, Joey reasoned.

"It's the fifteenth of November," said his mother.

The woman continued to stare, waiting.

Rhonda was shocked, unable to comprehend the woman didn't know what year it was, but she told her anyway.

"Oh, my," said the woman, her eyes wide at the wonder of it. "Later than I thought."

Rhonda stared at the woman curiously, as if she were unable to make sense of her.

Joey hung his coat next to his mother's. "Are you baking bread?" he asked. "It smells great." Joey admired the bulky wood-burning cook-stove in the kitchen. "Are you baking in that?"

"Oh, yes," she replied. "And it'll be ready soon!"

"Please," she offered, waving a hand at the stuffed chairs by the fireplace. "Sit and warm yourselves." She took a step back and added, "Oh, and where's my manners? My name's Ida Wheeling. That's what people call me. Ida." Her face radiated genuine hospitality, even as she regarded Max.

"Please make yourselves to home. I'm 'fraid you're gonna have to make do here for a spell. This storm's gonna get 'lot worse, 'fore it gets better." She smiled again, but this time, there was a hint of something, not exactly sinister, but far less benevolent. Joey noticed the smile didn't reach her eyes.

Rhonda gently took Ida's hands in hers. "I'm Rhonda Ingram. Thank you so much for taking us in. I don't know what we would have done if we hadn't stumbled across your farm. If we hadn't seen your light."

"Oh, honey, you're more'n welcome."

"I'm Joey." He introduced himself. He liked Ida very much. He saw kindness in her, and maybe more sophistication than he first thought, and certainly more than his father gave her credit for. Also, he loved how efficiently she'd dealt with his father.

"Good to meet you, Joey," said Ida, her warm smile dispelling all his harbored anxiety, like butterflies to the wind.

As Joey and Rhonda took the chairs near the fire, Ida stared at Max.

Max shuffled his feet, then hung his coat, gave a quick, uneasy smile, and nod at Ida. "Max," he said, curtly. "Thank you for your hospitality." Then he stood next to the fireplace to warm himself.

Ida shuffled into the kitchen and fussed with the stew on the stovetop. She added a few pinches of tan powder from an open canning jar before she was satisfied it was ready

Chapter 13

Max ate like a pig. They sat around Ida's table with the large blackened cast-iron pot set on a wooden cutting board. The steamy, luscious aroma of stew wafted from the pot, scenting the air with a delicate blend of wild herbs and the slightly gamey but enticingly savory smell of stewed venison. A golden loaf of freshly baked bread rested on a second cutting board, with a small crock of home-churned butter and a knife at its side.

Without restraint, Max ladled his stoneware bowl to the rim, sloshing some onto the table as he set it down in front of himself. Cutting a large chunk of bread and spreading a huge dollop of butter on top, Max dug in, slurping the stew and tearing into the bread with bared teeth, chewing noisily.

Rhonda stared at her husband in disgust, color rising in her cheeks.

Ida gave Rhonda a reassuring glance and a shrug.

Rhonda nodded gratefully and ladled stew into Joey's bowl and then Ida's, before serving herself.

"Thank you, honey," said Ida. She took up her tin spoon and dipped it into her bowl. She gently blew on the spoonful of stew until it was cool enough to eat.

"This is delicious," said Joey.

"Try the bread," said Ida. "It's my favorite recipe." She winked at Joey.

Joey smiled with a nod. He carefully cut a slice for himself and then spread a modest amount of butter on it. He took a bite of the hot, crusty bread, his eyes widening as he chewed and swallowed. The crusty bread held a heavenly soft, spongy interior that melted in his mouth. And the butter was like nothing he had ever tasted before, rich as a glorious spring day, and as creamy smooth as liquid sunshine.

Joey gushed, "This bread is amazing!"

"Oh, it really is!" exclaimed Rhonda, having taken her first bite.

Ida beamed. "Thank you so much. My mother taught me that recipe when I was just about your age," she said, winking again at Joey. "I surely do love a good sourdough."

"It's good," said Max, spilling food onto the table. He didn't notice and refilled his bowl from the pot.

Ida winced but said nothing.

They ate in silence for a few minutes before Rhonda asked, "Do you have any family visiting for Thanksgiving?"

"Uh, no," said Ida, a curious, quizzical look crossing her face. She didn't immediately meet Rhonda's eyes. "None of my family is left, that I know of." She took a sip of water from the tin cup by her bowl.

"So, you really live out here all by yourself? All the time?" asked Joey. He imagined the liberating freedom of it, his eyes bright.

Ida laughed. "Yes, it's just me. Has been for a long time. I don't mind, though," she went on. "I've got my animals to keep me company. And my work." She looked up sternly, shaking her spoon in rhythm with her words. "I don't think folks understand just how much sweat it takes to keep a place goin'."

"Don't you get lonely?" asked Rhonda, concern shading her eyes. "I can't imagine living so isolated, with only your thoughts for company." A hint of a shudder rocked her.

"Oh, I get by," was all Ida said on the subject.

"Doesn't make any sense to me," said Max. He wiped his mouth on the plain-weave napkin. "Seems crazy to stay out here and work your fingers to the bone for nothing." He was staring hard at Ida, some kind of challenge in his voice. "After all, what's the point? You're going to work your butt off, and then you're going to die. What kind of life is that?" The challenge had reached Max's dark, staring eyes.

Ida didn't rise to the bait. She regarded Max for a moment, then said, "I wouldn't expect the likes of you to understand. This is my *home*." The last word conjured the vast imagery of family, the toil and happiness of generations of lifetimes. "This is where my people are from. As far as I'm concerned, there isn't any place else to be," she finished earnestly, searching Max's eyes for an inkling of understanding. Finally, she shook her head and looked away, disappointed.

Max scoffed, "I bet people around here think you're some kind of old witch or something, living off the land all alone like this." He nodded to the ceiling rafters where bundles and bunches of herbs and plants hung from pegs to dry, as though that clinched it.

The hint of a smile crept onto Ida's face like a spider catching a fly in its web. Her leathery skin shining in the fire and lamplight, she replied, "Oh yes, some do."

"Max!" Rhonda was appalled. The courage to stand up to him had always eluded her before. But her outrage at his treatment of this generous woman who had taken them in from the cold—opened her home to shelter and feed them—was palpable now.

"What on earth has gotten into you?" she said, fear and resolve vied for dominance in her voice and on her face.

Max snapped his eyes to his wife, his lips flattening to a thin, cruel line. "I suggest you shut your mouth before you regret opening it," he spat, rising out of his chair to tower over Rhonda.

Rhonda cowered, and Max lurched as if to strike her. Joey jumped up, his chair legs skidding on the floor. He shot around the table to insert himself between his parents. His face was twisted in rage as he glared up at his father.

"Whoa there, little man." Max laughed at his son, his face turning dark. "Better watch yourself, boy, or I'm going to have to teach you some respect."

Joey didn't budge.

"I suggest you sit down, and keep your mouths shut," Max hissed. His fists balled at his side. Then something in his eyes changed, as if he'd come to a decision. They grew darker and bore into Rhonda's and then Joey's, until each of them looked away. Joey returned to his chair.

Max turned his glare on Ida. She sat quietly in her chair, her hands resting on the table on either side of her bowl. Her eyes locked on Max's as though she were sifting through his thoughts.

Rhonda fidgeted nervously, and Joey gawked, mesmerized at Ida's calm challenge to his father's threatening stare.

Finally, Max's smile returned with all its caustic, fraudulent bravado.

Ida's distaste for Max lay naked in her eyes. Her inner strength more than matched his physical threat.

Max blinked first. He looked out the window at the falling snow. He then relented and sat down at the table, his face calm and reflective. "Well, what's next? Anything for dessert?"

Joey felt deflated as the anger and adrenaline drained away, leaving him exhausted. He'd never stood up to his father before. But he'd been prepared to sacrifice himself for his mother's safety, disregarding his own. Still, something had shifted in his father. Some element of his behavior was fundamentally different now. Joey had never seen him so openly hostile toward them before in front of someone else. His father's secret self, the terrorist, had always been just for Joey and his mother. He obviously didn't see Ida as any kind of a threat, and that worried Joey. It was a dangerous shift.

"May I help you clear the table?" Rhonda asked. She tried to smile, her usual attempt to smooth things over, but failed miserably. She felt drained. Now that it appeared they'd be staying the night with Ida, Rhonda could hardly muster the energy to stand.

"Yes, thank you, honey," replied Ida. She scooted her chair out from the table and stood up.

"So, that's a, no?" said Max, sticking out his lower lip in a grotesquely childish display.

"What?" Rhonda asked. She stared at her husband like his head was on backward, not a clue in the world what he was talking about.

"Dessert. So there's nothing for dessert?"

Rhonda gaped at her husband as if he were a stranger.

"Nothing for dessert," confirmed Ida. She carried her empty bowl, spoon, and tin cup to the kitchen, where she placed them in the galvanized washtub on the counter.

"Very disappointing," replied Max. He stood, walked over to one of the stuffed chairs by the fireplace and sat heavily, shifting himself until comfortable. He stared into the fire, chuckling softly as flames danced in his eyes.

"Joey," said Ida, sweetly, "would you please carry the pot of stew out to the front porch for me?" She brought the heavy iron lid from the kitchen and set it on top of the pot.

"Yes, ma'am." His eagerness to help was the antithesis of his father.

"Thank you," she said. "There's a wooden box to the right of the door with a heavy hinged lid. Put the pot inside and close the lid. There's a metal latch; make sure it's tight."

"Okay, I will." The pot had cooled to the touch. Joey hefted it by the thick wire handle with both hands and carried it to the front door.

"Here, let me get that," Rhonda hurried over from the kitchen and opened the heavy door.

"Thanks, Mom," said Joey. He carried the pot out to the porch.

Rhonda closed the door as snow and wind swirled into the cabin. "It's getting pretty deep out there," she said to no one in particular, then walked back to the kitchen.

"Sure gonna to be a chore clearing the trail to the outhouse," said Ida. She glanced over her shoulder at Max, but he acted as though he hadn't heard her. She shook her head in disgust and returned to pouring hot water into the washtub from the large kettle she kept on the stove.

The cabin groaned in protest as a heavy gust of wind battered the walls. Rhonda jerked and stared up at the ceiling. As the wind rolled down the hollow, the front door thudded open. Joey dashed inside, snow coating him like freezer frost. Nestled in his arms was a small calico cat. He quickly closed the door and hurried to the kitchen.

"I found a cat!" he announced.

Ida turned quickly, relief washing over her face.

"Oh, thank goodness! Gigi, where on earth have you been? I've been worried sick." Ida gently took the bundle of fur from Joey. She sat at the table, holding the purring cat in her lap. She stroked Gigi gently, a gleam of iridescent affection sparkled in her crinkling eyes.

"She came right up to me on the porch," explained Joey. "I think she was down underneath, hiding from the snow."

"Probably right," said Ida with a laugh. "She doesn't care much for the snow once it gets above her head."

Max grunted with contempt, apparently paying attention after all.

"Fussing over a stupid cat," he said, shaking his head.

Ida scowled at the back of Max's head, sticking her tongue out at him. Gigi laid back her ears, her hackles raised along her back, and hissed at him.

Chapter 14

Max started into the fireplace, the radiant heat pleasantly roasting his face. The stuffed chair was surprisingly comfortable, fitting his body like the proverbial glove.

Marrying Rhonda had been a mistake. Her incessant chatter in the kitchen with Ida and Joey made him cringe. The sound of her voice grated like razors on his brain. She'd intrigued him, though, at first. That was how she'd tricked him into marriage.

She'd been one of those tight-twatted bitches who wouldn't let him into her pants on the first date. In fact, she'd held that back for the first two months. But he had to admit she'd been beautiful. Lovely long auburn red hair, something he had a weakness for. And her delicate, heart-shaped face, light hazel eyes, and full luscious lips—oh, those lips drove him crazy, made him dizzy with lust. That was the only reason he'd continued to pursue her. They'd met at the university they both attended.

When Rhonda first introduced him to Elizabeth, Max could hardly believe the two were related. They couldn't have been more different. Elizabeth was tall, by a good head over Rhonda. She had short, dark hair, a full wide face, and a husky build. She carried herself in an overtly masculine way that made her lesbianism obvious to Max. He didn't particularly care. The thought of sex with two women aroused him, though not with Elizabeth. She was too manly for his tastes. The realization that lesbians would have no interest in sex with him never crossed his mind. Their mutual disgust for each other was clear from the start. But he couldn't care less what Elizabeth thought. She was a freak of nature without value, in his opinion.

Joey's sudden shriek of laughter from the kitchen sent Max's skin crawling. So much like a little girl. Max's face grew hard. Only the image of beating the fuck out of Joey, teaching him what life would be like as a faggot—as if he were going to have a life—seemed to relieve some of the pent-up anger.

As a boy, Max endured his father's bullying. It was easier after his mother died. And as his own cruel nature blossomed, Max discovered he had a natural taste for it, a talent even.

Any suggestion that an innocent child remained buried in Max somewhere, would be a fallacy. Max never harbored that spark of innocence to begin with. The bitter loathing his father beat into him consumed any seed of humanity Max may have once possessed.

After Rhonda had finally "consented" to having sex with him, he'd realized later, the trap had been sprung. She was an animal in bed. There was nothing she wasn't willing to do for him. She'd debased herself in every way she could, doing anything he'd told her to do to hold his affection. It was a taste of what he'd hoped lay ahead for them. But after that first time, she'd reverted to her earlier chastity. Granted, that first time, he'd plied her with more alcohol than she had ever consumed before, greasing the wheels. But she was more guarded after that, wary, and refused all alcohol—she hadn't drunk since. But the promise of more was there if he would just commit to advancing their relationship to the next level. She'd never said marriage, but he understood that's what she wanted. She was very needy.

Rhonda began pulling away, sensing that he wasn't interested in anything more permanent between them. And, to his surprise, he couldn't stand the separation. He became angry and sullen, but understood that that sort of display would only repel her. So he swallowed his pride and proposed to her.

She'd cried and immediately said, 'Yes!'

It was the speed of her acceptance that now convinced Max he'd been played. His head swam in confusion as it dawned on him what this new life would be like: the loss of control of his own life, the responsibility and cost of supporting another person, the loss of freedom.

After the wedding, an intimate affair held at a small church with a few friends and family in attendance, they'd had the best sex of Max's life, and then no more. She'd become pregnant that first week of marriage and cut him off as soon as she realized she was with child.

It's uncomfortable, she'd whined. It was as though getting pregnant had been her only goal. And once she'd achieved that, carnal intimacy was no longer necessary. Like his needs didn't matter.

Grinding his teeth, Max seethed as his memories flowed through his mind like a rocky stream. He'd been doing that more and more of late, seething. His nerve was raised sufficiently now to finally overcome any misgivings, to do what needed to be done.

Soon after Joey's conception, Max had begun cheating on Rhonda. But when Joey was born, Max was the proudest man on earth. He'd stopped going to bars, and briefly grew closer to Rhonda again. But she seemed done with sex, and his frustration surged like a bore tide. And then, finally, he hit her.

Sweet catharsis!

A small slight and Max had exploded. His pent-up frustration and anger were released in a single moment of perfect bliss, approaching the ecstasy of orgasm. He was hooked like a junkie on heroin. His father's voice echoed in his mind from beyond the grave.

What took you so long?

Rhonda had shrunk inside herself a little more every day. Max threatened her with ever more severe punishment if she ever told anyone. And, of course, he threatened harm to Joey too, terrorizing her further still. He had successfully pounded into Rhonda's head that it was her fault he beat her. It was a delicate balance, though. He made sure not to leave marks where someone else was likely to see, and he became a master at taunting and belittling her until he had effectively broken her spirit, like a horse under a whip. It was his favorite sport.

After Joey was born, Rhonda didn't work. She had no escape. He discouraged her from associating with their neighbors, cutting her off from the outside world. And Max was thrilled at his power. But it was too much of a good thing. He couldn't stand to look at her anymore without total contempt swelling his heart. She was pathetic, a weak, broken thing. The feeling of entrapment engulfed him.

His love for Joey had soured to a bitter dusty residue when his son was ten years old. Max had begun having suspicions earlier, but when he'd come up with the idea of enrolling Joey in a local baseball program, Joey had tearfully refused. He whined that sports scared him, that he'd rather read books, and help his mother in their small garden in the backyard. That's when Max knew his son was a *faggot*. And then the pandemic hit, and the lockdown—six miserable months of confinement.

Max had begun sleeping around again, leaving Rhonda to cower at home in anticipation of his return. Occasionally, to reinforce his dominance—and just for the thrill of it—he'd rape her. But in his mind, it wasn't rape. After all, she *belonged* to him. But it had resulted in another pregnancy. He had to admit he'd handled that poorly, though it worked out in the end.

Knowing she was aware of his infidelity, he'd enjoyed inflicting the hurt of cheating on Rhonda. He did nothing to hide it from her. Eventually, he'd become bored with the whole situation and simply wanted out. He'd be damned, though, if he were going to leave Rhonda and still have to support her and her faggot son. That was never going to happen. That would be giving her everything he knew she wanted. That was too much for him to bear. He wanted her to suffer for his wasted time and money, the part of his life he could never get back. And then he wanted her and Joey dead, gone from his world, to no longer exist. The biggest mistakes of his life erased, a clean slate.

Max had his plan. The invitation to Elizabeth's house for Thanksgiving had been the perfect segue from desire to deed. There was going to be an accident. It was the ideal solution, a way that would leave him guiltless in the eyes of the law. After all, it wouldn't do for Rhonda and Joey to be out of the picture, and for Max to be stuck in prison for the rest of his life. He knew there would be an investigation into Rhonda and Joey's deaths. His bitch of a sister-in-law, Elizabeth, would make certain of that. But she was the one who gave them the back-road directions, and Max had every intention of making sure that was considered the reason for the fatalities—stranded in the wild, fatal exposure.

Now, though, the orchestrated accident he had been planning had shifted—with the snowstorm raging outside—to an act of God.

A satisfied smile creased his lips as Max stared into the flames.

Chapter 15

Ida watched Gigi eating from one of her dinner bowls set on the floor.

"Ma'am?" said Joey.

"Yes, honey? You can call me Ida. Everyone does."

Joey stepped closer, glancing over at his parents. They were sitting in front of the fireplace. His mother looked exhausted after helping clean up, and Ida suggested she go sit down.

"May I use your bathroom?" asked Joey.

Ida grinned. "Well, I don't actually have a bathroom. There's an outhouse 'round the side of the cabin. It's gonna be a real slog, though, through all this snow. But it's better than a shovel in the woods." She chuckled at the horror on Joey's face. "It ain't so bad. You do your business just the same as always. But be real stingy with the paper," she cautioned. "I don't have much of that left. When you're done, take a scoop of stove ash from the bucket in the corner out there and sprinkle it into the hole. Okay? That keeps the smell down."

"Okay," said Joey. He didn't want to go outside. What if that thing that chased them through the woods was still hanging around, just waiting for one of them to come out?

Ida could read the fear radiating off Joey like a billboard plastered across his face. She spoke confidently. "It's gone for now, Joey. Don't worry about that. You'll be safe."

He had no idea how she knew what he was thinking, but he breathed easier for her confidence and nodded. "Okay, thank you."

Ida smiled and nodded toward the door. "Go on then. Down the porch steps and 'round to the left. Careful in the snow."

Joey nodded, grabbed his coat off the hook by the door, and shrugged it on.

"Where do you think you're going?" Max turned from his revelry of the fire, giving Joey a disapproving glare.

Joey was used to the look. It had little effect anymore.

"The outhouse." He zipped up his coat and turned away from his father. He opened the front door to the snowy wind and darkness. Looking back at Ida, he asked, "Is there a light out there?"

"Sorry, honey. No light. You can prop the outhouse door open. There's a stick just inside for that. That'll let some snow light in."

Joey nodded. He didn't want to go out, but he didn't have a choice. He had to go badly. His guts were churning, an uncomfortable pressure building. Then it occurred to him.

"Dad, may I use the flashlight, please?"

Max didn't bother to look back at his son. "No. We need to save the batteries."

Rhonda shot a look at her husband, then turned to Joey with an apologetic gesture, as usual.

Joey stepped outside, pulling the door shut behind him. Warmth and light slid to dark and cold. The wind gathered and heavy snow continued. Joey strained to see ten feet in front of him through the swirling mass.

This is so not cool.

He pulled his hood up tight and traipsed through the accumulation on the porch, the snow squeaking like twisted Styrofoam as he walked. Nearly two feet of snow waited for him at the bottom of the steps. Listening intently, he detected no sound above the wind moaning through the forest. An ache in his gut spurred him forward.

Wading through the snow, Joey slogged around the cabin to the outhouse. *It's not so far.* He could just make out the small dark barn huddled under the deep snow a couple dozen yards behind the cabin. He could hear the faint gurgle of water and guessed there was a creek back there somewhere. Tramping down the snow in front of the outhouse, he swiped the remaining snow off the step with his foot. He reached up, grabbed the wooden handle, and pulled. The door opened easily, the long door-spring twanging as it stretched.

It was primitive, but Joey had no choice. He hurried into the squat little building. The bench was slightly higher than a regular toilet, but the function was the same. There was a round hole cut into the wooden bench. But there was no toilet seat, just the hole with worn-smooth edges. Seeing the stick Ida had mentioned, he grabbed it and propped it between the base of the bench and a shallow notch in the door, wedging it open about a third of the way. Joey's eyes adjusted to the subtle 'snow light' augmented by the gentle lamp glow spilling from the cabin's few windows, and he could see well enough for the business at hand.

He unfastened his pants and yanked them down, but just to his knees. When his bare bottom touched the cold wooden seat, his whole body rebelled, as a startled, "Oh!" escaped his throat. But as sweet relief flooded out of him, the cold was momentarily forgotten.

The wind surged in the treetops behind the outhouse. An invisible force suddenly descended like a hurricane, moaning, and shrieking its menace, loud and brutal as it approached. The outhouse shook, the wind pummeling the walls. The boards groaned, and Joey felt streams of air blasting through cracks between the rear wall planks. He hugged himself tight, squeezing his eyes shut until it passed.

A moment later, the dying wind retreated down the hollow, and Joey opened his eyes to the semidarkness. There was a catalog nailed to the wall to his left, its pages dried and crisp. He spied a half roll of toilet paper on the bench beneath it. He remembered Ida's warning.

I don't have much left.

He vaguely remembered jokes about using old Sears catalogs for toilet paper, but the idea horrified him. He opted for the real thing, but he used far less than he usually would have. There was no way to wash his hands, so he leaned over and swiped up a scoop of snow from the floor, and rubbed it vigorously between his palms. Then he wiped his hands on his jeans and called it good enough.

Standing, Joey pulled up his pants. His fingers were stiff with cold, and he fumbled with the zipper and button. Finally, he managed to fasten his belt. As he was about to take a step toward the door, an electrifying jolt seared his brain. Something splashed in the creek behind the outhouse. Then, the heavy stomping came, angry and determined. It thrashed through the snow outside. The echoing sound swallowed the world.

Joey's heart rocketed to a gallop in his chest. His blood ran cold. His body was frozen in place by the icy terror coursing through his veins. He began shaking violently but was unable to move his limbs. His breath came in great gasps as his body prepared for fight or flight, even as he struggled to move his muscles.

It thundered through the snow, like a team of Clydesdales stampeding toward the rear of the outhouse. Joey broke his paralysis in a sudden burst of determination and self-preservation. A jackrabbit breaking from cover, he leaped out of the doorway, kicking the prop-stick as he went. The door slammed shut with a bang as Joey hit the trail running.

Whatever it was gave chase. He heard it pounding after him. Racing toward the front porch, his heart thundering in his chest, the cold air tore at his throat as his breath roared in and out. His skin prickled and crawled in anticipation of jagged claws, or spear-like teeth, ripping into his flesh.

Rushing air-blasts of frozen breath coursed around him, a T-Rex sniffing its next meal. Mind-numbing terror froze Joey in his tracks. Squeezing his eyes shut, he waited for the final, awful moment. Hugging himself tightly, cringing in anticipation of his impending violent death, Joey waited. Then silence descended. The rushing air dissipated, sighing in disappointment.

Joey sprang into action and bounded up the steps to the porch, glancing to his right at the trail he'd made. There was nothing there. Panting from the heavy exertion, his sweat sour with fear, he stood silent and still. He could see the outhouse. The door was closed tight, the prop-stick lying on the step. The snow around the outhouse was white and smooth, undisturbed. His were the only tracks.

"What the hell?" Joey's mind swirled. It hadn't been his imagination. He was sure of it. It had been as real as the snow now coating his head and shoulders, as real as the cabin in front of him. He turned, his eyes following the disappearing outline of the trail he and his parents had forged earlier between the cabin and the forest. He could just make out the impenetrable wall of darkness that was the forest's edge. The wind lulled.

Trembling as the last of the adrenaline dissipated in his veins, Joey tried to compose himself. The trembling continued, but now it was from the gripping cold. Turning, he hurried across the porch, brushing the snow off his pants and coat as he went, forming his own micro-blizzard. Opening the cabin door, the welcoming glow of lamplight flooding out to wash over him, Joey rushed inside.

Chapter 16

"Oh good, you're back," said Ida, smiling.

When he pulled his hood off, Joey's reddish-blond hair stood in sweaty disarray on top of his head, his cheeks flushed radish-red, and his eyes wild. His breath came in gasps, like a marathoner at the finish line.

"What on earth?" Rhonda hurried over from the kitchen.

Gigi, curled on Ida's bed in the corner of the room, raised her head, her eyes narrowed in sleepiness. She studied the commotion by the door for a moment before settling back to her nap, purring lightly.

Max studied his son's face. He'd been silently watching Ida and Rhonda as they finished some chore in the kitchen. He was startled by the sheer terror on Joey's face.

"Joey?" said Ida. She hurried from the kitchen to join Rhonda at Joey's side.

"You told me it was gone!" stammered Joey. His hazel eyes were glued to Ida's and blazed with betrayal.

Ida recoiled from the slap of his words. She stepped back and wrung her hands in front of her as Rhonda worked to unzip Joey's coat.

"What did you see?" asked Ida. She stepped closer to Joey and placed a hand on his shoulder, as Rhonda slipped off his coat.

Joey stared at Ida, and then his eyes darted to each of his parents before finally settling back on the woman standing in front of him. His face calmed a degree, and he glanced at the floor as he spoke.

"Nothing," he whispered. His neck and cheeks were hot with humiliation.

"Nothing?" asked Max, incredulous.

Joey shook his head and looked up from the floor again, his eyes desperate.

"No," said Ida. "You wouldn't have."

Rhonda turned her worried look to Ida. "What does that even mean?"

Ida looked at each of them before resting her eyes on Joey again, ignoring Rhonda's question.

"But you heard it," she said. It was a statement, not a question.

Joey nodded, vigorously.

Ida leaned over and hugged Joey. He could smell wood smoke in her hair and on her heavy cotton shirt. When she stood back, she held him at arm's length.

"I'm so sorry, Joey. Truly I am. It's started."

Joey's eyes teared up. He hated that it was happening. He felt like such a baby. He shot a look at his father, and he winced at the disgust he saw there. He sniffled and wiped his eyes dry.

"What is starting!" shrieked Rhonda, her hands raised, splayed in exasperation in front of her.

"Come back to the fire," insisted Ida. She ushered Joey over to the warmth of the hearth. Rhonda reluctantly followed after hanging Joey's coat on a peg.

Max grunted in contempt and moved away as his son stood beside him. He returned to the stuffed chair he'd been sitting in earlier.

"What's all this nonsense?" he asked, adjusting himself in the chair, a tremor of unease in his voice.

Ida shot him a vexed look, then took the second chair for herself. Rhonda stood next to Joey, though she was already too warm. She ignored the discomfort and rubbed her son's arm.

"What you heard," Ida began, her eyes intent on Joey's, her voice calm but earnest, "was what my great-grandmother called the Teeka. She said it's what's kept these mountains 'round here so empty of folks. 'Cause they was so scared of it."

"Oh, for fuck's sake!" exclaimed Max, laughing and shaking his head. "What a bunch of hillbilly bullshit."

"Max!" scolded Rhonda, though her face betrayed her own skepticism.

Ida regarded Max curiously. Then a knowing smile crept onto her face, and she said, "*You'll* see."

Max stopped laughing like the flip of a switch. He stared at Ida in a challenge, but she kept smiling away. Finally, she dismissed him by turning her attention back to Joey.

"Don't know where it come from. My grandmother and other old-timers said that it's been here since the land formed, since life first started walking around. Others thought maybe it come into being when man did. Maybe it came as a way to balance things. Indians never settled here, neither. Somethin' kept 'em out, or scared 'em away. Anyhow, they knew better than to be here." She glanced at Rhonda and continued, "It never takes animals. Animals ain't good or bad. They just are. They live the way nature made 'em. It's always watching, though, for someone worthy to take away. It's what finally drove out the last of my people from here."

Joey's eyes grew large, his mouth dropping open in shock.

Rhonda gasped. "Oh, Ida! Really! I don't think this is helping." She looked at Joey, her eyes trying to convey a sense of order.

Joey knew Ida had been living out here, isolated from people, for a long time. He guessed his mother was wondering at the woman's susceptibility to all that loneliness. Certainly, all that isolation had left her reason vulnerable to old folktales. Surely, it must have affected her mind. Joey could see all that in his mother's face, but he didn't share her doubt.

Ida smiled sheepishly, but Joey knew that it wasn't at her own embarrassment. It was at his parents' foolish dismissal of the truth before them.

"'Course, I know y'all are from the city. You got all your modern things, and ways of thinkin'. Got no room for what's been here before. So I'll not take offense." Ida settled her eyes on Joey.

Rhonda fiddled with her hands. Ida caught the movement and nodded knowingly at her.

Rhonda blushed.

"When I said it's lookin' for someone worthy, I didn't mean what you might be thinkin'. Worthy to it means someone bad. Someone evil. It's here to pluck the bad from the place. That's what it lives on. It likes 'em cold and scared and guilty when it sucks out their essence."

Joey turned his horrified eyes to meet Ida's. "So, it thinks I'm bad?" His thoughts went straight to his friend Dennis back home and the things that his own heart told him it wanted, that it needed, what it knew to be right, natural. His father thought he was disgusting for being this way. Was he right? Was he really worthy of the beatings and ridicule his father dished out? Was he worthy of this thing's attention?

Ida gave a good-natured chuckle. "Oh, honey! I'd say you're the least worthy one here." She leaned forward. "But it doesn't know that till it gets a good whiff of you." She said this as if it were the most obvious thing in the world.

Joey was relieved. Rhonda was horrified that this old woman was filling her son's head with all this nonsense.

Max looked bored.

"You didn't see it," Ida finished, "'Cause it smelled you, and there wasn't any evil there." Ida turned and glared at Max. "If you see it, you know it's comin' for you."

"All right, I've had enough of this mumbo jumbo," spat Max, standing.

"Well, I think you're right, that's enough for tonight," said Ida, looking up at Max. "Would you fetch some firewood from the porch, please?" She smiled innocently at the muscular man standing before her, the request perfectly reasonable.

Max flinched, maybe because deep down he believed what Ida told them, but most likely because he felt it was beneath him, or because this ignorant woman was trying to order him around.

"It's gonna get real cold tonight," warned Ida. "Fire goes out, we might all freeze to death."

"Fine," said Max flatly, embers of anger smoldering in his eyes. Without another word, he headed for the door, catching the barest hint of a grin on Rhonda's face, presumably at his expense. And just like that, the rage flared, bright and fresh. He struck out, slapping Rhonda hard across her face, the sound of skin striking skin like a rifle shot.

Rhonda shrieked in startled pain.

"I'd wipe that smirk off your face if I were you," hissed Max as he grabbed his coat.

"Oh, honey!" exclaimed Ida, rushing to Rhonda's side.

Shocked at the viciousness of Max's attack, Rhonda held a hand to where Max had struck her. Tears trickled from her eyes from the pain and humiliation.

"Bastard!" screamed Joey. The lid on his anger exploded, and his rage at all the injustices perpetrated by his father boiled over. Joey ran at his father, his fists swinging wildly.

The first punch landed hard against Max's lower back, a startled "Oof!" escaping the burly man. The second punch landed as Max spun around, his balled-up fist connecting with his son's cheek with a resounding SMACK!

Joey flew backward and crumpled to the floor, staring up at his father. Boiling hatred blazed from his eyes. He panted in frustrated rage, the pain from the strike not yet registering in his brain.

Rhonda rushed to her son, kneeling at his side. She pried his hand away to inspect the damage Max had done. Joey's cheek was split open just below his eye and was already beginning to swell. The cut was small but ragged. Rhonda shot to her feet.

"You fucking monster!"

Max looked at his wife and laughed in her face.

"Save it, you fucking cunt," he said, opening the front door to go fetch firewood, slamming it behind him.

"Come sit at the table, Joey," said Ida, helping the boy to his feet. "Rhonda, there's a fresh towel there by the washtub. Pour some hot water on it and bring it over here, please?"

Rhonda sighed, then hurried into the kitchen and did as Ida asked, the pink handprint clear on her pale face.

Ida got Joey settled in one of the dining chairs and went to the rack of shelves above the counter next to the cook-stove. She scanned the shelves, then retrieved a canning jar of clear liquid and carried it to the table.

She grimaced as she tried to twist off the lid, and she held it out to Rhonda. "Could you open it, please? My hands ain't what they once was."

Rhonda traded the dishtowel for the jar. Ida took the towel and gingerly dabbed at Joey's cheek.

"Ow!" Joey winced as the hot towel touched his broken skin, but he didn't pull away.

Rhonda easily opened the jar and sniffed the contents. She detected a faint astringent odor. "What is this?" she asked.

"Witch hazel," answered Ida, holding her hand out for the jar. "'stilled it myself. It'll clean the cut out real good."

Rhonda handed the jar to Ida.

Taking it, Ida pressed the towel against Joey's cheek under the cut. "Tilt your head to the side," she instructed.

Joey complied. Ida tipped the jar just enough to allow a brief thin stream of the clear liquid to run across the cut. "Gonna sting a bit," she said as Joey flinched at the quick, sharp pain.

Ida dabbed at Joey's cheek, then examined the injury. "Gonna swell some, but the bone ain't broke," she reported.

The front door burst open, and Max lumbered in carrying an armload of split firewood. Gigi hissed at him from the bed, then settled down again—but she kept a wary eye on the man.

Ignoring the cat, Max slammed the door shut with his foot. He trailed snow across the floor as he carried the firewood over to the fireplace and dumped it on the dwindling pile already there.

"There's your firewood," he snapped. He returned his coat to the hook by the door. "Bet you get a shiner from that," he said to Joey. A spiteful grin twitched his lips as he watched the others.

Ida studied Max's face. After a moment, a knowing grin briefly graced her lips, her eyes glistening.

Joey watched his father too.

Max quickly turned away from Ida. He seemed weak-kneed and unsteady, like he might collapse. Ida grinned at him, but Max didn't see it. He stared at the flames dancing in the fireplace nervously shifting on his feet as if unsure what to do.

The throbbing in Joey's face grew steadily as the shock and numbness of the punch faded.

"Be right back," said Ida. She carried the towel out the front door. She returned seconds later, twisting the edges of the towel, now filled with snow to form an ice pack.

Rhonda hovered near Joey, but her angry eyes never left her husband.

"Hold this on your face for a bit," said Ida, handing the snow-filled towel to Joey. "It'll help bring the swellin' down."

"Thank you, ma'am," Joey gingerly pressed the towel against his cheek. He winced at the cold, but the deep throbbing pain began to subside almost immediately.

Ida smiled at him. "You'll be fine." She patted Joey's arm.

Rhonda yawned, drowsiness weighted her eyes as exhaustion overwhelmed her. They were not getting out of here tonight. Elizabeth was going to worry about them, but Rhonda couldn't do anything about that.

After the scare with Joey, she had to admit she was now frightened to go to the outhouse. She knew it was stupid. The Teeka was nothing more than an old wives' tale, silly folklore to scare children. Yet her reluctance was nearly paralyzing, and she had to get over that because there was an ocean in her bladder pressing hard against the dike.

"I'll go with you," Ida said, looking at Rhonda with open amusement.

How did she do that? But she was grateful. "Thank you," she said and went to get her coat.

"Where are we sleeping?" asked Max. He scowled at Ida's double-size bed in the corner of the room, settling his eyes back on their host.

Ida didn't even look at him. "Upstairs," she said, her head tilting toward the steep stairs at the far corner of the cabin. "There's a lamp up there already. Three beds." She followed Rhonda and retrieved her worn sheepskin coat from its peg by the door. Then she pulled on her leather hat, looking like a scarecrow come to life.

Rhonda wondered if Ida had been expecting them. Why else would she light a lamp in the attic? Rhonda now realized this was the light they saw in the forest. She wondered how such a faint light could carry so far through the woods. She had no answer, so there was no sense pursuing it. They were here and that's all that mattered.

"Come on, Joey. Let's go check it out," Max said, walking to the base of the stairs—like he and his son were best friends embarking on an adventure together.

"I'll wait here," said Joey coolly as water dripped down his arm from the melting snow in his compress. Then he looked to his mother and Ida. "I'm sorry," he apologized. "I was scared and ran out earlier. I forgot to put ash down the hole." The blush rose quickly, coloring his entire face.

"Frozen by now," Ida said.

Rhonda opened the front door, and the two women stepped out to the porch. Snow blasted into the cabin on the swirling wind until the door closed with a thud.

"Whatever," said Max. He climbed the creaky steps up to the attic.

Joey heard the floorboards creak in protest as his father walked around above him. There was a pause, and then the groaning of bed ropes stretching as his father tested one of the beds. Then more footsteps across the ceiling as he tried the other two.

The fire had died to coals. Joey hoisted himself up from the chair and walked to the kitchen. He set the ice pack in the empty washtub and returned to the fireplace. He'd never dealt with a real fireplace before. They had one in the living room at home, but it was gas—instant flame at the flick of a switch. He realized now there was no comparison to the real thing; the quality and abundance of heat, but also the work to maintain it.

He lifted the iron poker from its peg next to the fireplace. He'd only ever seen one used on TV or maybe in the movies. He poked at the charred logs on the blackened iron grate, adjusting them with quick, deft movements. The fire responded with surging flames, air reaching the freshly exposed wood surfaces.

Joey smiled in satisfaction, confidence growing in him. He set the poker back on the peg. Hefting a couple of the logs his father had just carried in, Joey nimbly set them onto the flames.

Feeling pressure on his leg, Joey saw Gigi slinking against his ankle. Purring quietly, she cast affectionate winks up at him.

"Well, hi there," he said, gently stroking the thin calico cat.

Gigi gave a quick, quiet, "mew," in response.

Joey sank into one of the stuffed chairs, the flames in the fireplace growing with the addition of fuel. Gigi rubbed against his leg a few more times before jumping up and settling into Joey's lap.

Rhonda and Ida returned, a blast of wind and snow shrieking into the cabin to announce their arrival. Joey's eyes shot open, his drowsiness whipped away with the wind. He hadn't realized how tired he'd become. The look of petrified terror on his mother's face froze his heart.

Gigi watched the two women but made no move to leave Joey's lap.

"Well, well," said Ida, beaming at Joey. "Looks like you two are old friends."

Chapter 17

Rhonda hung her coat. Her eyes were dazed as she walked over and sat next to Joey.

Ida, still cloaked in her coat and hat, said, "Joey? Could you help me outside? I need to get out to the barn and break the ice in the water trough for Sugar and Oats, my cow and horse. I'm certain it's froze over by now."

Ida might as well have dumped a bucket of ice water over him. Joey's eyes shot wide open in sudden terror. He did not want to go back outside. "Uh." His eyes darted from Ida to his mother, hoping she would offer a reprieve. She didn't. She smiled, though it was fleeting, trying for a measure of reassurance that failed.

"It's okay," Rhonda coaxed, without conviction.

Joey's earlier experience consumed his thoughts, no matter how hard he tried to block it. But he trusted Ida. He knew there was something out there, the Teeka, but she said it had already smelled him, and he wasn't in any danger. That it had passed him by. But that didn't ease his fear.

He had an epiphany then. His panic turned to understanding, a dawning comprehension. He'd been so frightened for himself that it hadn't occurred to him until now. If *it* really existed, it was likely after his father. Joey knew in his young heart that it couldn't be his mother it was searching for. His mother—the only one who ever stood between him and his father. The only one until now. The memory of his father returning with the firewood clinched it, because Joey was quite sure his father had seen something.

"Okay," he said as he shifted in the chair, trying to gently dislodge Gigi from his lap.

"Scoot, Gigi," said Ida, shooing at the cat.

Gigi startled, stretched luxuriously, and gracefully jumped to the floor. She sauntered back to Ida's bed where she snuggled herself down on the quilt, a purring ball of calico fur.

Joey walked to the door to get his coat. Shrugging it on, he said, "I'm ready." His face was serious, his brows knit together like he was about to embark on a death march or a security patrol behind enemy lines.

Ida chuckled.

Max descended the stairs, stomping with each step. Scanning the room, he noted Joey and Ida near the door. "Going somewhere?"

Rhonda spoke up. "They're going to the barn to see to Ida's cow and horse."

Max laughed. "What the hell could they possibly need?"

"Water," spat Ida. Then her lips curled into a smile devoid of mirth or humor, as welcoming as a sharpening stone to the steel of an axe blade. "Would *you* rather do it? It's not a complicated chore. I'm sure you could manage."

Max's face flushed. His eyes narrowed, and with his mouth pressed in a tight, thin line, Max looked at Joey and said, "No, I'll leave the chores to the womenfolk." He dropped into the chair Joey had just vacated. "By the way," he continued, "those beds are certainly a stretch of the word. They're not very comfortable. You might want to upgrade at some point."

"You're welcome to sleep in the barn with the animals," Ida shot back, reaching for the door handle. "Though, I'm not sure you'd be very good company for my Sugar and Oats."

Joey giggled.

Max scowled, his bitterness poisoning the air around him, like a sour odor.

Joey followed Ida out the door and closed it behind them.

Rhonda said nothing. She knew better. She busied herself studying the jars of plant powders and crumbles, seeds and nuts, and mysterious liquids on the shelves next to the cook-stove. From here, she'd be able to watch Joey and Ida's progress from the small window above the stove, at least what was possible through the falling snow and twilight darkness. A quaking shiver trembled through her body. Her outhouse experience played through her mind on a loop.

Chapter 18

Rhonda insisted Ida use the outhouse first. It was polite. It was her house after all, and she was older, though Rhonda marveled at how spry she appeared, despite her apparent age—which she couldn't quite pin down. In one moment, Ida seemed ancient and at others like a woman Rhonda's age of thirty-five. She guessed life in the woods took its toll and Ida was younger than she looked. She wasn't going to ask. Regardless, Rhonda could hold it a bit longer, a little bit longer.

"Thank you, honey," said Ida, in what was becoming a familiar term of endearment, as she stepped down from the outhouse.

"Of course," said Rhonda. She stepped aside, allowing Ida to pass. Then she entered the outhouse, closing the door behind her. She had her jeans unfastened practically before the door was shut.

Oh! It's so cold! The wind clawed at the eaves, buffeting the small building. Rhonda could feel tiny slivers of icy crystals stinging her face. Finally, her stream started, the relief enormous.

"I don't know how you do this all winter long," Rhonda called out, tapping her foot nervously.

There was no response from Ida. Rhonda assumed she couldn't hear her over the howl of the wind, which was growing by the second.

Another sound crept to her ears then, but it couldn't have been Ida. It came from the forest behind the outhouse. Her heart sprinted in her chest as she recalled Joey's experience.

"Ida!" Rhonda shouted, abandoning any attempt to conceal the fear bleeding into her voice.

The noise came again, steadily now, large and heavy. Something was tramping through the snow behind the outhouse. And getting closer. Whatever it was, its progress was unaffected by the depth of the snow.

"Ida!" Rhonda screamed. She imagined some awful giant beast smashing Ida to the ground in one devastating stomp, reducing the woman to a mound of pulp.

Again, there was no response.

Unable to control her violent shaking, a mantra of, "Oh fuck, oh fuck, oh fuck," escaped Rhonda's lips while she stood and yanked up her pants. The stomping was thunderous now. The building shook around her as each step fell closer to the outhouse.

Rhonda steeled her nerve to fling the door open and run to the cabin, but she was too late. Whatever it was, it had arrived. It stepped up to the back of the tiny, flimsy building and stopped. There was a moment of quiet, then a soft sound of something running a hand or paw over the boards at the back of the building. Then a heavy snort burst out, as though it were sniffing the air, testing her scent, undoubtedly finding it more complex than Joey's.

Rhonda hadn't believed Ida's story of the Teeka. How could she? It was ridiculous. She'd rationalized it as folklore. People living in rural mountain hollows, isolated from civilization, believed all sorts of things. Any educated person would reject these beliefs straight away. With her heart thudding in her chest, Rhonda knew she'd been wrong. It didn't matter how it was possible. She believed the story now.

The booming stomps resumed, and Rhonda abandoned any thought of fleeing to the cabin. Whatever it was, it moved quickly. It was directly in front of the building now, the thin boards of the door the only thing between them. There was a smell, too. It wasn't the outhouse smell—a damp sourness. This was different, heavier, dank, and rotten. Rhonda reached out to lock the door and realized there was no lock. Although she couldn't see the wooden handle attached to the door, she felt it. There was no latch of any kind. She grabbed the handle, the wood cold and rough in her hand, and held on with all her might. She expected it to be ripped out of her hand, the door flying open, some indescribable horror standing there, then lunging at her with sharp, horrible teeth to tear her apart.

But nothing happened. There were no more sounds, and the smell dissipated.

She held the door handle for what seemed like an eternity. At last, she began to relax. Her fingers were stiff from the cold and the force she'd used from gripping the handle. She took several deep breaths, the frigid air raw in her throat. With a whimper she forced herself to give the door a slight push. It opened hesitantly, the door spring complaining as it stretched.

There was nothing there. The path looked just as it had when she and Ida stood out there a few minutes before. The snow was unmarred and smooth, save for her and Ida's tracks. There had been nothing else there.

Rhonda laughed nervously at her foolish imagination.

Silly me.

She stepped hesitantly down to the path, anticipating something rushing at her from its hiding place, out of the sky for all she knew. But all was quiet. Even the wind had died down. The snow fell heavy around her in great, abundant flakes. She took a couple of steps along the path to the cabin. The outhouse door slammed with a resounding bang behind her.

"Ida?" called Rhonda. "Are you there?"

"Yes, honey," came the reply.

Rhonda saw her now. Ida stood on the cabin porch, watching her.

"I'm so sorry, honey," Ida said, dropping her gaze to the ground.

Rhonda was about to speak when the odor returned, suddenly overwhelming. The air was thick with it, thicker than the snow. And then she felt a hurricane rush of air as some force roared toward her. Rhonda thrashed in a circle as crashing footsteps dashed at her, but she couldn't see anything, couldn't even tell which direction it was coming from. But it was upon her.

Rhonda screamed as she flailed, throwing her hands up to repel whatever attack was coming. She fell to the path, eyes squeezed tightly shut, holding her hands to her head to protect herself.

Then, the sounds ceased. The wind tugged at Rhonda's hood, and she shuddered. Her terror ebbed away in pulses, and she was left exhausted and whimpering in the snow. She was startled by the footsteps approaching her, but it was only Ida hurrying to her side from the porch.

"I'm so sorry, honey," she said again. "Couldn't be avoided."

She helped Rhonda to her feet and held her in a hug, until the violent spasms racking her body calmed down.

"It's okay now. It's okay," cooed Ida. "It doesn't want you."

Rhonda's face was expressionless, her eyes aimless. Her legs were like jelly as Ida helped her along the path to the safety of the porch.

"That just leaves Max," Rhonda said as they climbed the steps.

Ida looked her in the eyes and nodded. "That's right, honey."

Chapter 19

Bundled in his coat, hood drawn tight like an arctic explorer, Joey spied his father's footsteps leading to the woodpile at the end of the porch. A splattering of yellow snow beyond the porch's edge indicated where his father had relieved himself. Joey scanned the area near the cabin, but falling snow hid almost everything behind a curtain of shifting white and graying darkness beyond. The trees at the edge of the property were lost from sight. The yellow light from the window was pale and anemic against the cold, expansive darkness.

Ida stepped carefully through the five or six inches of snow that had drifted under the porch roof. She tugged an old shovel leaning against the cabin wall from the grip of the snow. From the shape of it, Joey thought at first it might be for shoveling feed. It looked like a giant scoop. But he realized now it was for shoveling snow. From his harrowing trip to the outhouse earlier, he knew it wasn't a great distance from there to the small barn, maybe twenty yards. But it stood at the edge of the trees, and he was frightened by what might be hidden there in the gloom—a primordial fear passed down from man's earliest existence. His heart thumped heavily in his chest, his hands tingled.

"I'll let you handle this," said Ida, handing the shovel to Joey.

"Okay," he said, taking it. It was heavier than he expected, but he thought that was a good thing. It would make a good weapon.

"We can start at the outhouse," Ida said, indicating that Joey should go ahead of her.

"Yes, ma'am." Joey started down the steps. The cold stung his face—the cut from his father's punch throbbed painfully. But after a few minutes, the skin numbed and any discomfort ebbed away, like the tide retreating from the shore.

Fresh snow accumulated in their previous footprints to the outhouse. As they tramped along, Ida casually asked, "Joey? Are you frightened of your daddy?"

The question startled Joey. It embarrassed him too, probably because of the answer. His friends weren't terrified of their fathers. It wasn't supposed to be a normal thing. But it was his only experience as far back as he could remember.

As uncomfortable as it made him feel, Joey nodded and said, "Yes." His voice was quiet and almost lost in the wind, its pressure increasing, the storm growing stronger.

"I'm awful sorry 'bout that," Ida said. "It shouldn't be that way."

They shuffled the last few steps to the end of the trail. The barn lay dead ahead, barely visible through the haze of falling snow. Joey knew what to do now. He shot a look over his shoulder to make sure Ida wasn't standing too close. Then he began to scoop out a narrow path with the shovel. As he hefted each shovelful, the wind caught the loose powder and blew it in great streaming clouds, a shifting scrim of angel's wings and bridal veils across the field. If he'd had a sturdy broom, Joey thought he might be able to sweep the path clear. As it was, the shoveling went quickly, and they made their way to the barn at a rapid pace.

Sugar must have heard them approaching. As they drew near the barn, she released a series of soft moos in anticipation of their arrival. Accompanying Sugar came the occasional nickering from Oats, the horse.

"There's a door, there to the side under the lean-to," said Ida. "Shovel to that."

Joey nodded. A few feet from the door, Joey felt the tightness in his muscles from the unaccustomed work. His ears pricked up and a shot of adrenaline surged through his veins. Something had moved in the forest behind the barn. He could hear the gentle gurgle of the creek and was sure the sound had come from the trees on the other side of the flowing water. It had been a single *flump*. It could have been a buildup of snow suddenly dropping from a high branch to the soft cushion of snow on the ground. But he didn't think so. There was something deliberate about the sound that caused Joey to freeze.

From behind him, Ida quietly said, "It's okay, Joey. Just finish to the door so we can get inside."

Was there a shade of fear in her voice? Joey couldn't be sure. But her intent seemed clear. Get inside as quickly as possible.

He didn't need any further prodding. He redoubled his efforts. Sweat beaded on his face, trickling into his eyes. He finished the path to the side door and wiped his face with his coat sleeve. As he reached for the handle, there was a second *flump* from the trees. More deliberate this time, and closer.

"Pull the cord," Ida whispered.

Joey could just make out the woven cord hanging out from a small hole in the door next to the wooden handle. He pulled the cord and felt it give with a clunk as the latch inside lifted up, releasing the door. The door glided inward on rusted hinges with a long low moan.

Ida gave Joey a nudge, and he hurried into the barn. She quickly followed behind him and immediately closed and latched the door.

Ida was breathless. "Well now, that was somethin', wasn't it?"

From the opposite side of the barn, Sugar let out an ear-piercing bellow. A heavy thump and squeak of wood sounded out as her shifting bulk pressed against the stall boards. Oats seemed less interested in their arrival. The barn was cold, but the smell of manure was strong and fresh.

"Smells like we got here just in time," said Ida.

"Was that *it* again, the Teeka?" asked Joey.

Ida laughed, a high, sharp sound. She laid a hand on Joey's shoulder. "No, honey. It was just the snow falling. But it was excitin', wasn't it!" She laughed.

Joey cringed. He didn't think it was funny at all. He was terrified. "I thought it had come back for me," he said. He felt betrayed by Ida. He'd trusted her. He'd really known her only a short time and realized now that his trust might have been misplaced. Maybe she was crazy. The thought flared bright in his mind, a roman candle of revelation. This woman lived out here in the middle of nowhere by herself. How could she not be crazy? His fear swelled anew. He'd been terrified of something out in the woods when maybe what he should have been afraid of was right here in the barn with him.

Joey could hear Ida moving around. She released a latch and flung open a hatch door covering a window. The darkness in the barn receded slightly—enough that Joey could see more of the interior of the barn. He could see the dark slats of the three stalls along the back wall. Sugar stood in the end stall farthest from the door, a hulking dark shape. She leaned against the stall gate, facing them. Her eyes were dark, shiny pools in the shadowed interior, watching them. Oats was in the center stall, next to Sugar. He regarded them a moment, then returned to whatever horses pondered.

Ida made her way back over to Joey. "I'm sorry if I scared you," she said softly.

Joey didn't respond. He didn't know what to think about her. He backed away a step or two as she approached him.

"I weren't bein' cruel," she said, "At least, I wasn't meanin' to." She paused for a moment. "It's always around," she explained in a low voice. "But it's already judged you and found you good, sweet-hearted. It only wants the ones with bitter hearts, shriveled things full of hate and evil. That's what it likes, must taste good to it."

She reached out and took Joey's hands in her own. Joey didn't pull away. He wanted to trust her. He wanted to believe that he was safe. But he found everything she'd told him harder to believe now. He'd had no problem believing her earlier, right after his terror at the outhouse. But now he questioned the memory, doubting if it had really been the way he remembered it at all.

Ida squeezed his hands. But when she spoke next, her voice turned dark. "It is out there. It was there while you were shoveling. It's there now."

Joey listened for sounds beyond the wind howling and whistling through the trees. But he heard nothing. He shivered, the hairs on the back of his neck stood on end, as if some ancient instinct was telling him there *was* something outside the barn. The roller coaster of emotions exhausted him. The notion that some vague menace was hiding in the shadows, or behind some shield or veil, guarding its presence from observation, was too much for him to understand.

Joey felt tears sting the corners of his eyes. In all his thirteen years, he couldn't remember a time when he wasn't frightened of something. And what he feared most of the time was his father. He'd been frightened of his attraction to Dennis, too. But that felt right. He knew in his heart that it was. This latest fear was too much, though.

"I was having a bit of fun," said Ida. "I sure didn't mean to hurt you. That noise was falling snow. I see now I shouldn't have teased you that way. Even at my age, I sometimes do things I regret, and I'm sorry, Joey."

Joey couldn't help himself. It was her admission of fallibility that swayed him. He hugged Ida. Frustration and helplessness escaped his lips in a sob as his tears moistened her coat. "I believe you." His voice muffled against her shoulder.

"I'm scared," he whispered. "My dad wants to hurt us," he confided. "I think he wants to kill us." Joey took a sharp breath. The incomprehensible was out now. He'd understood for years that his father loathed him, despised him and his mother—the beatings and scorn were certainly a big clue. But it wasn't until this trip that he truly understood the depth of blackness in his father's heart. When his parents chatted and laughed in the car, Joey could see the falseness, the darkness in his father's eyes in the rearview mirror. His mother had seemed oblivious to it or was simply ignoring it. The way she always did. Joey felt embarrassed at the acknowledgment, though he wasn't sure if it was for his mother or himself.

To Joey, his father's eyes were dark pits of calculating hate. Exasperation at his mother's inability to see it evaporated when Joey suddenly realized she wasn't really looking at his dad, her husband. She was looking at the fantasy of the husband he never was, the one who laughed, like he had back then, who chatted and made plans for the future. She didn't see that he was simply lulling her into a false sense of security while he plotted against them.

It was a horrifying realization to know his father wanted them dead. Joey's heart constricted. He struggled to catch his breath. Searching his memories, he could see his father's total contempt for his family. It was evident in his every interaction with them. He marveled at how blind they'd been to it. So, what Ida said next wasn't such a shocking thing.

"I know, honey. I could see it in his eyes from the moment he first stood on my porch."

Joey heaved a sigh.

Ida patted Joey on the back, then pulled away and held him at arm's length.

"A person's true self is usually right there in their eyes. You have to look beyond what they want you to see and stare deeper into what's really there. Not easy most times, people can be tricky about that. But it wasn't hard at all with your daddy. He doesn't feel threatened here. He doesn't feel the need to hide it here." She thought over what she'd said and then shook her head. "Grab that splittin' maul over there in the corner; we need to break the ice in poor ole Sugar and Oat's water trough."

At the sound of her name, Sugar mooed loudly, the sound emphatic and penetrating, filling the small confines of the barn. Oats swung his head around and stared at the cow.

Chapter 20

Max stared into the leaping flames in the fireplace, the light dancing across the hearth in a dazzling spectrum of yellow and orange. His brow creased in thought, Max considered his options. He was committed to the outcome. There was no question about that. He was giddy at the unexpectedly perfect situation he now found himself in. His mind raced to a future where he lived his life with the joy of self-gratification, no dead weight sucking the passion out of his existence. He chuckled at the unintended pun. *Dead weight.* His wife and son were nothing but old baggage requiring disposal.

Thinking about his parents, Max knew that his own father felt the same way about Max's mother. She was a weak, small woman devoid of imagination or passion. It was no wonder his father beat her. She'd obviously deserved it, with her pathetic cowering and pleading. Probably for the best, that she developed pancreatic cancer when Max was thirteen, the same age Joey was now.

When his mother died, Max remembered the renewed devotion of his father to him. They never mentioned his mother. He instinctively knew that his father never wanted to speak of her again, so Max stifled any positive memories of her. It wasn't hard for him to do. The attention from his father may have been rough, especially when he drank, but it was given to him in an effort—on his father's part—to mold Max into a real man, a man just like him. A chip off the old block.

Joey would never be a real man. Queers weren't men. Simple laws of nature dictated that. Joey would always be Max's greatest shame. It was plain as day that that gene came from Rhonda; it ran in her family. Just look at Elizabeth. A fucking dyke! Max wondered if Joey was his son at all. He looked nothing like Max and everything like Rhonda. Could she have slept around behind his back? He considered it only a moment before dismissing the idea. She wouldn't have had the nerve.

He wanted to smash her. He wanted to shred both of them into oblivion. He was beginning to get an erection.

Grunting a chuckle, Max shot a look over his shoulder. Rhonda was staring out the window in the kitchen. She couldn't even let Joey go out and water the fucking livestock without hovering.

"See anything interesting?"

"They're still in the barn," Rhonda replied.

Rhonda avoided looking at Max. She'd considered going out with Joey and Ida rather than staying inside with *him*. She wished she had. Something had changed, blooming like an oil spill, coating the atmosphere around him. His anger was oppressive. Her own sister had been trying to convince Rhonda to leave Max since the day she met him. But the thought of losing him had been unbearable. Whatever he did, she'd convinced herself in her heart that he'd loved her. She'd been certain of it.

IDIOT! How could you have believed that?!

She hadn't been able to hate him even when he took out his frustration and fury on her in the form of beatings. *The baby!* Her mind had repeatedly called out in vain.

But he'd grown far more abusive with Joey now, and Rhonda couldn't ignore that. And she couldn't forget the life insurance policies either. He wasn't just dangerous now—he was homicidal. She needed to get Joey away from him—and now they were stranded with him in this little cabin in the middle of nowhere.

Elizabeth's directions had proved to be terribly flawed, possibly fatal Rhonda realized. She didn't understand how her sister could have been so careless. Rhonda felt a spark of anger at Elizabeth, but it quickly faded.

I probably read the directions wrong.

But she knew she hadn't.

Damnit! She'd paid excruciating attention to them.

And yet here they were.

They were stranded here, for the night at least, and Max made his peace with that. The snow was only getting worse. Their car was stuck. But, he thought, all was not lost.

The strange thing was, being stranded miles from anything, Max felt a surge of freedom. There was no threat from Joey or Rhonda, and certainly not from Ida. He laughed at the idea that any of them could stop him from doing whatever he wanted. *Punishment is coming.* Oh, he was enjoying the pictures in his mind. Hard creases folded the skin of his face into a sadistic grin. His eyes were bright and glistening in the firelight. He couldn't just kill them all outright. It had to look like an accident. He stared hard at the fire, as the plan finally coalesced in his mind.

"Any sign of them?" asked Max.

"No," said Rhonda.

She'd been lost in her thoughts and hadn't really been looking at anything. But now she focused on the dark, faint shadow of the barn and didn't see any movement, save the falling snow.

My God, so much snow.

Her chest felt tight in a claustrophobic grip, the air in her lungs stagnant, refusing to flow. She was suffocating on fear. She'd never been one of those people who romanticized the notion of being snowed-in somewhere, all cozy and warm. The thought made her shudder, want to scream. And here they were, in this fucking snow globe from hell.

Taking several deep breaths to purge the grip of her panic, Rhonda was startled as Max's voice whispered into her ear.

"I'm going to rape you now."

Before Rhonda fully registered Max's words, he seized her arms. He flung her toward the table where they'd eaten dinner just a short time ago. Her arms reached out to catch herself, her open hands skidding across the rough wood of the tabletop.

"What are you doing, Max? Stop it! They'll be back soon!" She staggered but regained her balance and turned, holding her hands out to thwart her husband's advance.

A sadistic leer stretched over Max's face. "This is where the real fun starts," he said. His voice was gravelly and hoarse with excitement. He charged toward Rhonda, grabbed her outstretched arms, and whirled her around. He enveloped her in a crushing bear hug, forcing the air out of her lungs.

As Rhonda struggled to breathe, Max forced her jeans down below her hips, the still-fastened waistband digging painfully into her skin, abrading her hips raw.

Rhonda struggled with every ounce of strength she could, but there was no thwarting Max. She felt his heart pounding against her as he locked her in his powerful arms. Arms she had once marveled at for their muscular beauty, now forced her to bend over the table. He easily held her in place with one hand while he unsipped the fly on his pant's with the other.

"No!" screamed Rhonda.

"I hope this hurts," growled Max.

"No! Stop it!" Pain seared inside Rhonda. Her mind shut down, the cabin fading, she went limp. She was a rag in Max's hands.

Max felt her go loose. Bitch, he thought. But it wasn't about the sex for him. It was about possession and asserting his authority over her. It was about humiliating her with the knowledge that every part of her belonged to him. And it was about hurting her. He quickly reached his climax, even as he was losing interest in the act.

The funky, sour smell of Rhonda's fear that had excited him a few moments ago now sickened Max. As he buttoned up his pants, he said, "You stink. Better clean yourself up. They'll be back soon."

Chapter 21

The ice shattered like glass as Joey hammered the splitting maul down into the water trough. The temperature was in the low twenties, and there was only about a quarter of an inch of clear ice coating the water. He broke it up into big chunks with the maul and then set the heavy tool aside.

Reaching into the frigid water with his bare hands, Joey pulled out the larger, slippery chunks of ice and tossed them out the window Ida had opened closest to Sugar's stall. Then he went back for more.

Ida led Sugar out of her stall and left her to wander around the barn as she used a pitchfork to clean out the soiled straw, pitching the waste out a hatch in the back wall and onto the compost pile. She finished the chore by shaking handfuls of fresh straw across the stall floor, like a shaman performing a ritual.

Sugar stood a few feet behind Joey, chewing her cud and watching as he cleared the ice out of her water. He'd pressed himself against the wall when Ida first opened the stall gate and the heavy animal ambled out. But Sugar just sniffed Joey's coat and walked away.

"Ice is all out," said Joey.

"Thank you, honey," said Ida. She finished shaking out the fresh straw and brushed off her hands and pants. "Can you start mucking out Oats' stall next? Just open the gate—he won't hurt you." She inclined her head toward the pitchfork she'd leaned against the wall.

Joey found he was less frightened of the horse than he had been of Sugar. "Okay," he said.

Oats sniffed Joey's hand as he reached for the gate latch. It reminded him of the Teeka sniffing him. But he wasn't frightened now. He opened the gate and took up the pitchfork. Then he entered the stall. Oats watched him passively, stepping to the side as Joey opened the hatch in the rear wall of Oat's stall. Then, the horse plodded out into the barn and joined Sugar.

"Come on, Sugar," Ida said. She made a clicking sound with her tongue.

Without hesitation, Sugar lumbered back into the stall and sniffed the fresh straw, then went to the water trough and lowered her head, taking a long draft of the ice-cold water.

Ida broke off a single flake of hay and dumped it into the slatted feeder at the side of the stall. Then she swung the gate closed, latching it snugly.

"That should hold her over till morning," she said, satisfied. "She'll need milking then too. You can help me with that if you'd like."

"Sure," said Joey, not sure what milking entailed, but happy to help out.

When they were done repeating the whole process in the horse stall, Ida sat back on a wooden bucket momentarily catching her breath.

"Are you okay?" Joey was worried she'd overtaxed herself.

Ida waved her hand in the air. "I'm fine. I usually spread this work out a bit more, but with all the snow, I figured we ought to get it done quick."

Joey nodded.

When Ida finally stood up, she said, "I guess we should shovel out to the chicken coop while we're out here, so it won't be so deep in the morning. And by we, I really mean you." She looked out the open window near Sugar's stall. "I 'spect we're in for another foot overnight by the way it's comin' down now."

"Really? Wow, we're going to be here for a week!" Joey found the prospect exciting. Only it would be better if his father weren't with them, and the Teeka wasn't lurking out in the woods. Joey was surprised to find the Teeka didn't frighten him anymore. He'd passed that test, and Ida had assured him it wouldn't come after him again. Still, he'd prefer it didn't hover around anymore, thank you very much.

"It could possibly be a week," said Ida. Her smile was guarded before her face went neutral again, but it was lost on Joey in the dark interior of the barn. "Let's get that trail shoveled and get back to the house. This cold is startin' to sink into my bones." She closed the wooden window covers, making sure they were latched tight.

Joey shoveled a trail in front of the barn. The chicken coop squatted about twenty feet away between the barn and the garden fence. Ida closed the barn door and followed close behind Joey. She smiled at the boy's enthusiasm. It was always nice to have agreeable company.

"I know you're scared of your daddy," she confided. "I can help you and your mother. But we'll have to see into his heart first. We have to know that he can't be saved."

Joey didn't know what to say. He suspected when she'd said "we" that she was referring to herself and the Teeka. Or maybe she was referring to himself and his mother. Snowflakes landed on his eyelashes as he looked at Ida. He brushed them away. Finally, he nodded and turned back to shoveling the last few feet to the chicken coop.

"Do we need to feed and water the chickens?" asked Joey.

"No need," replied Ida. "They're roostin'. Tomorrow will be soon enough."

Together Ida and Joey trudged back to the cabin.

Chapter 22

"Oh my, that was cold!" exclaimed Ida. She and Joey stamped their feet outside the front door and entered the cabin in a flurry of wind and swirling snow.

Joey quickly closed the door behind him. As he unzipped his coat, he noticed how quiet it was in the cabin. Tension filled the air. It lay as thick and heavy as the fallen snow outside.

Max sat by the fireplace. He was staring into the flames in smug satisfaction. Joey couldn't figure out what the cause of such contentment might be, but it couldn't be good, and he was immediately on guard.

Joey spied his mother huddled on the small wooden chair by the closet door under the stairs. She was as far from Max as she could be without going up to the attic. The glow of lamplight barely reached her, but Joey knew by her slumped posture and hitching shoulders that something had happened. Something bad.

"Mom?" squeaked Joey, his voice catching in his throat. He shrugged off his coat, letting it fall to the floor.

Rhonda didn't respond. She sat with her arms wrapped around herself, staring at the floor. Joey rushed to her side.

"What's wrong, Mom?" He was afraid to touch her. Was she hurt? He could see that she was crying softly. She was lost in her own thoughts, unable to hear him or at least unable to respond.

Indecision flustered Joey and a hot anger rose up inside of him. He glared over his shoulder at the back of his father's head, knowing without doubt he was to blame for whatever this was. Kneeling in front of his mother, Joey reached out. He held his mother's hands, waiting for her to come back to him. It scared him how far away she was. She might as well have been on the far side of the moon.

"She's just being dramatic," said Max, from his chair. He didn't bother to turn around.

Or maybe she's afraid, thought Joey, shifting sideways to look at his father.

"What did you do?" Joey's accusation elicited a tiny flinch from his father. But he made no reply.

Joey turned back to his mother, speaking softly. "Mom? Can you look at me please?" He was near tears himself. He couldn't count how many times he'd seen his mother cry, but she'd never been so withdrawn from him before. A tumultuous kaleidoscope of anger, fear, and desperation churned in Joey's heart like a raw stew. He felt his blood pressure rising, his heart pounding.

Ida watched them for a moment. She made no comment. She hung her coat, then retrieved Joey's from where he'd let it fall to the floor and hung it next to hers. Placing a hand on Rhonda's shoulder, Ida stooped slightly and spoke to her gently.

"Rhonda, honey? I'd like you to drink some tea, okay?" Ida straightened and stared with an intensity that should have caused Max's head to burst into flames. To Joey's disappointment, it didn't.

Ida looked across at Joey, whose eyes were locked unwaveringly on his mother. "Joey, honey, go add a few small pieces of wood to the fire in the cook-stove, won't you please? It's the small door at the top, under the kettle."

Joey hesitated then looked up at Ida, her solemn face peering down at him.

"Yes, ma'am."

"Going to spoil her, giving in to all of her histrionic bullshit," Max spoke over his shoulder, his voice a master class of indifference.

Joey didn't think that was true—that his father was indifferent. He detected something else there, just under the surface. Maybe it was fear, or uncertainty. Maybe he knew that this time he'd gone too far. Joey had never heard a tone like that in his father's voice before. It worried him because he couldn't imagine what his father might have done to feel that way.

Max recovered from his momentary lapse of resolve. "She's just ashamed because she liked it so much," he laughed.

The implication was crystal clear. Joey was outraged at his father's callous cruelty. However, nothing surprised him, not after the years of mental and physical abuse at the hands of that monster.

Joey caught Ida's gaze. She nodded at him, to gather a few pieces of firewood from the box next to the stove.

Opening the small firebox door, he used one of the sticks to stir up the coals, then placed the new pieces inside and closed the door.

"Open the little vent at the bottom of the door," said Ida. "That'll let the air in."

Joey did as she instructed. The effect was immediate. The flames flared and crackled in the firebox as they began to consume the fresh supply of wood.

"Thank you, honey," said Ida. She turned her attention back to Rhonda.

Joey noticed the empty chair next to his father but decided to sit at the table instead. He didn't want to be any nearer to him than he could help.

Ida managed to get Rhonda to respond. She cupped Rhonda's quivering chin in her hands, speaking so softly that her words were nearly lost to Joey.

"Come sit at the table with Joey and me," she said. "We'll have some tea before bed. It'll help you sleep. And I promise it will help settle you inside too." She glanced down into Rhonda's lap.

Rhonda hiccupped a few more sobs, then settled down. She let go of Ida's grasp and wiped at her eyes. She tried to smile but settled on resignation instead. It seemed the best she could do.

"That's better," said Ida. "I know you probably can't believe it right now, but things are gonna be alright. I know 'bout family strife." She paused, unbidden memories flashing through her mind, the hatred and violence too much to bear. "My sister once hurt me real bad. Hurt me to my core. Still haven't recovered from it. But there's always tomorrow."

Rhonda didn't believe things would ever be right again. How could they? Max was going to destroy her and her son, and if Ida wasn't careful,

Max would destroy her too. Rhonda accepted all of this. Her decision to leave Max had come too late. She'd always thought she deserved no better life than this. It was her own prophecy fulfilling itself. But Ida's smile, so open and comforting, wedged a sliver of hope in her mind, just enough to let in a tiny beam of light, a sunbeam through the storm clouds.

"Don't you worry none," confided Ida. "I've been around an awfully long time, and I ain't gonna let nothin' more happen to you. You need to understand that, alright?"

Rhonda wanted to believe her more than anything in the world, but how could she? She'd been under Max's tyranny for so long, she couldn't even remember what it felt like to be unafraid, to be free, really alive, and not just surviving from one violent moment to the next. She wanted to believe Ida, but she couldn't make the leap of faith. Not yet. But she smiled a weary smile, still more hopeless than cheery, and nodded.

"That's my girl!" beamed Ida.

Rhonda laughed spontaneously and startled herself. She covered her mouth—she felt out of control of her own emotions and her life. She was close to breaking down into hysterical guffaws or maniacal shrieks. Then she looked into Ida's soft pale-blue eyes and any lingering fear evaporated. There was a strength in Ida's eyes that took Rhonda's breath away."

"No more," whispered Ida.

Rhonda was captivated. She nodded that she'd heard, that she understood, and that she believed.

"That's my girl," Ida said again. "Now come along and sit at the table with Joey and me. We'll have a real nice cup of tea before bed."

"Yes," said Rhonda, a smile creeping onto her face, but it was a timid thing ready to dash away again at the first sign of trouble. She let Ida guide her to the table, grimacing at a stab of pain inside from Max's assault. Ida helped her down into the chair opposite Joey, with her back to Max.

"Thank God you've finally stopped all that fucking sniveling!" exclaimed Max, casting a withering stare at his wife, his eyes blazing with contempt.

Joey and Rhonda cringed at the sound of Max's voice.

Ida had had more than enough of Max's bullying. She'd been about to mix up their tea, but she changed course and stormed to the front door with purpose. She darted a dark stare at Max as he sat, legs splayed as though he were king of the castle. She scoffed and reached for her shotgun in the rack above the coat pegs. She lowered it to her shoulder, turning and taking aim at Max.

"I think you might be more comfortable in the barn," she said. "You've 'bout wore out your welcome in my home."

"Whoa!" yelped Max, his hands flying up in a gesture of surrender. The smug look on his face was gone, replaced by a look of fear. He smiled nervously, looking around as if she must be talking to someone else. But she wasn't, and he knew it.

"I'll not have such disrespect under my roof," growled Ida, her arms steady as she kept the barrel of the gun aimed at Max. "Do. You. Understand. Me?"

Max was a smart man. He knew when it was time to change tack. He nodded in understanding, although an edge of contempt still marred his conciliatory frown. "Yes, ma'am," he said, and dropped his head in shame. But he wasn't fooling anyone.

Ida didn't budge. "Good," she said. "I'm sorry to use such a harsh method of gettin' your attention, but I wanted to be sure you realized just how serious I am." She looked over at Rhonda and Joey, both staring in rapt attention at their new hero. Then she shifted her eyes back to Max. "You're all welcome in my home 'till this storm blows over. That's the neighborly way I was raised. But I'll not tolerate any more of your bullying. It's unsightly, and I'm tired of it."

"I understand, and I'd like to apologize for my...disrespectful behavior." He lowered his hands, palms out toward Ida in supplication.

"Fine," said Ida, grinning. She lowered the shotgun. "Well, I'm glad we got that settled." Then she strolled back to the kitchen, taking the shotgun with her.

Max shook his head—he was going to play the good guest for now.

Ida didn't buy Max's act for a minute, but she'd made her point and was convinced he would behave himself for the time being, and that was all she needed.

Max took the poker from its peg and poked at the dying embers in the fireplace. Sparks spewed up the chimney. He re-hung the poker and set three fresh logs onto the fire.

"Thank you, Max," Ida said from the kitchen.

"You're welcome, Ida," he replied. "Don't want to freeze tonight." He sat back down watching the flames catch and spread.

"No, indeed we don't!" she agreed.

Rhonda's mind was spinning. She was certain Ida was going to shoot Max. And when she didn't, she was sure that Max would rush her as she returned to the kitchen. But he didn't. And now she didn't know what to think. The fight in Max seemed to have left him, but she knew better than to believe he'd surrendered. Max didn't give up, ever.

Joey watched as Ida gathered several jars, their contents a mystery, and four heavy stoneware mugs from her kitchen shelves. He felt a nudge. He looked down as his mother rested her hand on top of his, a timid smile flickering on her face.

Joey smiled back, cheered to see his mother coming out of her despair. They sat quietly as Ida busied herself with the tea.

Ida hummed as she worked, some old-timey song with a lilting Gaelic quality to it. It was the one her mother sang while she worked in the kitchen. Ida couldn't remember the words anymore, so many years had gone by, but the gentle melody, soft and somber, soothed her like nothing else could.

The shotgun lay across the back of the counter, as Ida poured boiling water from the kettle. Misty spirits of steam rose from each mug. She prepared four small piles of herbs on a narrow wooden board. It had small depressions carved out of its surface for measuring. She filled two tea infusers, small double-sided orbs of silver hinged in the middle and covered with a decorative pattern of tiny holes to allow the water to pass through. They had belonged to her grandmother, and she cherished them. Scooping one side of the orb into the carved depression in the board, she then flipped the other half over in a practiced motion, snapping it shut and trapping the tea inside. Each infuser had a delicate chain attached at one end. She dropped one in each of two mugs to steep, draping the fine chains over the rims.

Reaching to the top shelf, Ida took down a one-quart pottery jar with a bark brown glaze. The lid had a small knob on top. She set the jar down near Joey and Rhonda.

"Just a minute more," she said with a smile.

The aroma of the strong flowery chamomile tea wafted through the air.

"Oh, that smells wonderful," cooed Rhonda. "I haven't had chamomile tea in years."

"There's a patch at the edge of the field I always harvest from," confided Ida. She lifted the infusers from the mugs and flipped them open over the waste pail at the edge of the counter, tapping them to knock out the spent tea.

"Here you are," she said, setting the mugs down in front of Rhonda and Joey. She took the lid off the pottery jar and set it down on the table.

"Honey," she said. Then she retrieved two spoons from the wooden drain-rack on the counter, laying one next to each cup.

"Thank you, Ida," Rhonda said.

Ida's eyes sparkled. "Drink up! You'll sleep like a baby."

Joey and Rhonda helped themselves to the honey as Ida repeated the process and waited for the second round of tea to finish steeping.

"Oh! Just heavenly!" exclaimed Rhonda after her first sip. "I've never tasted a better cup of chamomile in my life."

Ida tapped out the dregs from the second round of tea. "Nothin' beats homegrown."

"Max?" said Ida, pleasantly. "Would you like honey in your tea? I recommend it; it rounds out the flavor just right."

Max had been silent since their confrontation. He replied with a calm, friendly tone, "Sure, why not."

"All right," said Ida. She carried his cup to the table and dripped a spoonful of honey into it, stirring gently.

Rhonda got up to serve Max his tea, but Ida shooed her back to her seat. She handed the cup to Max. "Here you are."

"Thank you," he said, taking the cup. A genuinely pleasant look of surprise crossed his face. "Mmm, this does smell good!"

"Enjoy," said Ida as she retrieved her own cup from the counter.

Settling into a seat at the table, Ida indulged in a small dollop of honey too, stirring it into her tea as she looked from Joey to Rhonda. "I think this is just what we all need to settle in for a good night's sleep." She took a sip and winked at Joey and Rhonda.

Chapter 23

Max set his mug of tea down on a small table. He slumped in his chair. Something was wrong. He didn't feel right. He felt like he was being smothered under a mound of pillows. His eyes darted around the room in a panic, his vision was blurred and distorted, images slurring together.

Joey and Rhonda sat at the dining table watching the heavy snow falling from the dark sky. The wind howling at the eaves of the cabin. The tea seemed to be having the desired effect on them both. They each felt more relaxed than they had since arriving at the cabin. A drowsiness consumed them, and Rhonda felt a warming sensation throughout her lower body, the pain from Max's assault melting away.

Ida watched Joey and Rhonda. They seemed lost in thought. She shifted her eyes to Max. Although his back was to her, she could see his head beginning to dip as he fought the growing tug of sleep.

"Time for bed," announced Ida, setting her still full mug down and rising from her chair.

The sound of her voice jolted Rhonda out of her private reverie. Blinking and shaking her head to clear the cobwebs from her mind, she smiled almost drunkenly at Ida. Joey startled too, as if surprised at his surroundings. Max was still lost in his own thoughts, though his head had stopped nodding like the prow of a ship in rough seas.

Ida smiled—pleased they'd reached this plateau. She gathered up the three mugs and carried them to the kitchen and set them in the washtub.

Rhonda and Joey stood up and gathered their strength for the migration up to the attic and the beds that awaited them.

Ida stirred the coals in the fireplace before adding two more logs to the glowing bed of embers. The fire caught quickly, the growing flames casting brilliant yellow light across the hearth and Max, who sat dazed in his chair. His eyes were wide open, captivated, hypnotized by the dancing flames, his pupils huge like black saucers. His face was slack and blank like a slab of raw meat, his mouth hanging open.

Lifting his head, he gazed up at Ida standing before him as if surprised to see her there. Then his face slid into a glowering sneer as he tried to force his lips to speak.

"Cat got your tongue?" asked Ida. A Cheshire cat grin spread rapidly across her face.

Max stuttered several times. A trickle of drool escaped from his mouth and dribbled onto his shirt. He seemed completely unaware of his surroundings, as if his head was full of wool. Finally, he managed to project a grunting sound from his throat, but it was an unintelligible grouping of vowels and consonants that made no sense.

Ida laughed. Shaking her head, she said, "I think you'd better get up to bed now. We don't want you falling asleep down here. You'll be so much more comfortable upstairs."

Max tried but was unable to speak, as he was carried away on waves of oblivion.

"Not much of a tea man, I guess," Ida said, enjoying the moment.

Reaching out with heavy, clumsy arms, Max clutched at Ida's hand. But his aim was off, and his fingers curled on empty air. His face puckered with frustration at his inability to seize her. "What did you give me?" he finally managed to stammer, though it came out as, "Whhhaahdyoivee?"

"Oh, hush now, Max," said Ida. "Just a little something to help you relax, to take the edge off. You got a real problem with your anger. I'm going to help you with that."

"Biiiccch," he stammered.

Ida smiled again. "You may be on to somethin'."

Rhonda and Joey staggered up the stairs like zombies in an old black and white horror movie.

"I'll see that Max makes it up to bed. Sleep well."

Stretching out on Ida's bed, Gigi mewed, her eyes soft and loving.

"Long night t'night, Gigi. You go ahead to sleep now."

Gigi tucked her head between her delicate paws and closed her eyes, her tail curling across her nose.

Ida blew a kiss to the cat and walked back to Max.

"Here now," she said, standing in front of Max. "It's time for you to get upstairs too. Don't want you sleeping down here tonight. I need you to be up there with your family."

Max stirred from his delirious fugue. He seemed to recognize Ida, and he stiffened as she bent to grab his hands in an effort to pull him to his feet. "Drrruugd mmee," he managed to spit out.

"Well, we couldn't have you hurtin' anyone again, could we?" she replied as she took hold of his limp hands.

Max tried to shake Ida's hands away, but he couldn't manage it.

"Now now, none of that. If you concentrate on standin' up, without all that fussin', you'll do all right," coached Ida.

Max managed to stagger to his feet, swaying dangerously, yet finding enough of his center to keep from toppling over.

"Good boy," said Ida, as if she were talking to a puppy that had just learned to pee outside. "The first few steps will be the hardest, but you should be able to find your stride after that. Come on, take a step."

Ida held Max's hands, leading him along through his first clumsy efforts. "Good!" she cheered, after Max took several successful steps, managing to make it around the chair and toward the stairs. "You'll be up in your bed sawing logs in no time."

Max wanted to lash out at Ida. He knew she'd put something in his tea, but he was helpless to fight back. Bed was his single purpose now. Sleep. He couldn't focus. His vision was as blurred as melted candle wax, no solid lines to anything. He felt dizzy and was certain that if the force holding his hands, leading him forward, were to disengage, he would reel off the cliff he was edging along.

"Take a step up," came Ida's voice, through a vale of fog.

Ida slowly led Max up the steps and across the attic floor to the bed at the far corner of the room, her brother's old bed. She stopped him at the edge of the bed and let go of his hands. Max fell backward onto the bed, the ropes protesting with mighty squawks, his weight straining every fiber. Ida gathered up Max's legs hanging over the side of the bed and swung them up and over so that he lay fully on the thin mattress. She untied his shoelaces, pulled off his boots and set them under the bed.

There was a blanket draped over the foot rail and she drew it up to Max's chin, then turned and repeated this for Rhonda and Joey, both far away in sleep now.

Standing at the top step, Ida looked back at her three guests. She could see snow falling outside the small window, but heat from the fireplace downstairs had warmed the room.

As she started down the stairs, Ida whispered, "Sweet dreams."

Chapter 24

The fire burned high, drawn by the raging wind like a tornado up the chimney. Then it settled until the next gust battered the cabin. Ida took down a small wooden box from the top shelf in the kitchen. She held it tight as she lowered it to the counter and lifted off its fitted wooden lid. Setting that aside, she reached in and drew out a small woven bag. She loosened the strings that bound it and opened it gingerly.

Reaching into the cloth bag, she took a small pinch of the dried, flaky contents, careful not to take too much, mindful that she mightn't wake up again if she did. She sprinkled it into her mug of tea. "That ought to be enough."

Wiping the tarry residue from her fingertips onto the dishcloth, she retied the bag and returned the wooden box to its shelf. Ida stirred the mixture in the mug with her spoon.

Ida sat down in her favorite chair. Staring into the flames, she braced herself for what was coming next. With the last visitors, eight years earlier—or any of the others before—she hadn't made it this far. She'd realized early on they weren't worthy. She'd prepared an alternate tea, and when they became confused and forgetful, she'd sent them on their way out into the night to find their fate. She'd kept their backpacks, though, finding all sorts of useful items: toilet paper—a miracle invention in Ida's opinion—the shotgun and a box of shells.

This time, she was certain this would be the last time. She lifted the mug to her lips and gulped the liquid down, causing a spate of coughing. The leaves and ground roots scratched her throat and required a moment or two to swallow completely.

Ida leaned back in the chair. The warmth spread throughout her body.

"Alright," she whispered, a tremulous note of hope floating through her voice. "It's time."

Chapter 25

Ida settled back in her chair. She felt the warmth of the fire on her eyelids. The aches and pains that were her constant companions suddenly evaporated and she now felt as serene as a baby at rest. Lost in her own thoughts, Ida bathed in the embrace of warm summer yellows, slow-moving rivers, and memories of scented flowers. She smiled, but then a darkness fell—a dark stain spread slowly across her thoughts. It lazed there until the warm summer yellows faded, and the slow-moving rivers ran the color of clotted blood.

Ida started panting as memories of her sister, Eugenia, flashed through her mind. Eugenia screamed at Ida, the fury of her temper, a sharp punch to her soul. She'd loved Eugenia once. Ida could never hurt her. But Eugenia accused Ida of stealing her husband's affections. It wasn't true. Ida couldn't have done that. Her heart was held tight to another, in a forbidden devotion, its very existence taboo yet undeniable in its strength and solidity.

Maggie.

Eugenia struck out with fury, and Ida's heart sank in sorrow.

Noise, abrasive and distracting, flooded her mind, and she couldn't make sense of it. She was lifted to a quieter plane, where her memories came back to her in fits and starts. Ida found herself sitting in a summer field, the field outside the cabin. Around her streamed hazy but clearing visions from other minds. She recognized each as a member of the family that had come to her, desperately seeking shelter.

Each family member's memories were projected into her mind. Clear and sharp at first, then fading away into blackness. Ida felt nothing until a burst of memories and emotions pulsed around her like bubbles— white and yellow and red and black, serenity and love and pain and death.

Ida focused on Joey's memories, until his thoughts and feelings were clear in her mind.

Rhonda figured prominently in Joey's thoughts. His love for her was palpable. But a thread of disappointment wove through the fabric of his thoughts, like a thread of black silk twisting through a field of gold. Disappointment in his mother, that she couldn't bring herself to save them from his father. And there was another love, smaller, less defined, budding. A boy at his school. *Dennis.* Young love! But those feelings were tangled with strands of fear. Bullying and self-doubt. But what featured most in his mind was his father, Max.

Terror!

Joey thrummed with the sharp, blackened metal threads of fear. He feared for his life and the life of his mother. Flashes of violence flared around Ida, a fireworks finale of anger. Max is beating his son, threatening his son, terrorizing his son—these were his longest-lasting memories.

Pain.

Ida saw the moment with Joey in the bathroom when his father, in anger and disgust, pushed Joey beneath the water. Ida gasped for air as if Max had attacked her too. The threats, rather than the physical abuse, seemed more damaging. The flashes in Max's eyes were clear. He meant it. One day he would kill them.

Ida turned away from Joey and focused on Rhonda's memories, so dark. She lived in the black of hopelessness. Her worst fears were her everyday companions. The sinking, plunging feeling of absolute sorrow staggered Ida so completely that she felt her own heart shrink away from it.

Ida saw Max raising Rhonda's hopes, then dashing them away with a furious rage that cast her ever farther down into the depths of despair. She was a drowning woman grasping at the light above as she sank into oblivion. She saw a black hole in Rhonda's heart.

And yet, blended in with the pain, were silky threads of happiness. The brightest being the day Joey was born—joy at the new life she'd given birth to.

An infinitesimal thread of silky sky blue skirted the others. It was a new thread of hope, freedom. She had been planning to leave Max on this very trip. She and Joey were going to live with Rhonda's sister, Elizabeth. But the thread dwindled to nothing at Ida's cabin, the hope of escape ending with Max's rage at Joey's blooming nature and his brutal assault on her just a short time ago. But she returned again and again to that dark void.

A flicker of vision, a glimpse, a tiny plea, a cry of mourning, *my baby!*

And Ida knew. Her heart thudded with dread at the implication.

Max frightened Ida. His stream was the color of blood, fresh and bright, arterial, blended with dried smears of dull rusty brown, ugly and sickening, foul. His entire being was engulfed in anger and hate. Ida shied away, protecting herself from the assault of rage. It brought to her mind the approach of a terrible storm, an earth-shattering quake, an inescapable flood, roaring toward her with no sure footing of higher ground to save her. There was no safe harbor to shelter from the all-consuming storm of Max.

Memories of Max's father, rough and mean, were woven with Max's own hate, rage, and angry desire. There was no light in his river of life. Everything was dark and ugly. He thrived on it and drew sustenance from its darkness. Max wanted to be free of his family, the family he saw as his greatest mistake, a bitter burden to be buried and forgotten. He saw them as the only thing standing in the way of his bigger life, a life of unfettered hedonism, exquisite carnal gratification. His due.

Then Ida saw that moment in the living room when Max dug a black hole, that bottomless mineshaft of grief in Rhonda's heart. Rhonda was pregnant and cowering from her husband, a tiny shrunken form. He's standing over her, larger than life in his own mind. Max's fury beating like a black heart. Furious at his entrapment, certain in his heart that Rhonda had become pregnant again to strengthen the tether holding him back, chains binding him to her pathetic life.

Ida watched as Max ran at her, drawing back his fist and launching it at her swollen belly with the force of the accumulated rage of his entire life. It ended Rhonda's pregnancy, and the life growing inside her died with that act.

A final thread of memory caught Ida's attention. It caused a rush of adrenaline as she recognized herself among Max's thoughts. It was no surprise or shock Max regarded her with as much disdain and contempt as he did his wife and son. He saw her as an obstacle to his plans to eradicate Rhonda and Joey from his life. But he'd been thinking about that a lot. He had a plan to deal with all of them.

Before, he had planned to disable his family with broken bones and let them freeze to death in the woods. But Joey had seen Ida's light, and that had saved them. Now she saw his plan to trap them in the attic and set fire to the cabin. That had been his plan for this very night. She saw his vision of himself, standing outside with the shotgun trained on the cabin, watching the inferno consume his family's lives. Ida felt nauseated by his glee.

Ida had seen all that she needed to see. There was no longer any doubt in her mind that Max was the most worthy she had ever encountered.

She descended back into herself. Gradually she felt the warmth of the fire in the hearth, heard the wind screaming in the eaves, and felt the weight of Gigi climb into her lap, a purring ball of comfort.

Chapter 26

Ida gently stroked Gigi's fur. The cat softly purred, a soothing vibration. Ida stared into the flames—she judged time solely by how far the logs had burned down while she was away. She guessed about an hour or so. She didn't own a clock, never had need of one, for her concept of passing time was fluid. She knew when it was morning and time to feed the chickens and milk Sugar. She knew when it was midday and time to eat her noontime meal. And she knew when it was night and time to put things to bed, and, of course, milk Sugar again. She had little need to be more specific than that. She did her baking by sight, smell, and experience.

Ida felt no urgency to thwart Max's plans. He would sleep through until morning—she'd made his tea potent enough to ensure that. Her course of action was obvious to her. There was little she needed to do to prepare, save one important chore. She gently woke Gigi. The cat jumped down to the floor.

"Sorry, sweetheart." She hefted herself up from the chair and shuffled over to the kitchen. Rummaging through the cabinet below the shelves, she drew out a length of coiled rope, its fibers tight and strong. She closed the cabinet and took her sharpest knife from the block on the counter.

Ida drew out and deftly used the knife to cut two, five-foot lengths of the tightly twisted cord. She rewound the remaining rope, put the knife back in the block, and returned the diminished coil of rope back in the cabinet. The room spun as a sudden bout of dizziness disoriented her as she stood. The residual effect of the tea was not unexpected, and not particularly pleasant, either.

Ida rested her hand on the counter to steady herself. The after-effects of the strong tea coursed through her, then receded. As she waited out the faintness, snippets of her own memories slinked through her mind.

Eugenia was so angry about something Ida had never done. The truth was that Eugenia's husband, Evan, had a notoriously wandering eye. But

Ida was not at risk to his temptation. Her heart belonged to Maggie, though it was to remain forever hidden. Maggie shared Ida's attraction, confiding that her heart raced whenever they were near, but the consequences were too severe to tempt either woman to more than stolen afternoons together. Theirs was a May-September affair, as Maggie was many years younger than Ida. But Maggie had been the first to approach, and Ida never stood a chance against her heart's desire.

The rage in Eugenia's heart brought Max to the forefront of Ida's mind. They were nothing alike, and yet Eugenia had had a streak of fury in her bordering on lunacy. The smallest perceived slight could never go unpunished, tenfold in scale. And when she'd convinced herself that Ida tried to steal her husband, hell itself could not have mustered a more hideous retribution.

Ida was startled by her own tears. She thought she would have been immune after so many years. She wiped them away. "It's done," she said quietly. She shook her head and gathered up the two lengths of rope from the counter. Then she climbed the steep steps to the attic. She tried to push thoughts of Maggie from her mind, but they still snuggled gently in her heart. It was time to focus on the matter at hand.

As she neared the top step, Ida heard the wind howling outside, but there was something else there too. She knew what it was, but she'd never heard it so aggressive before. Scratching and shrieking blended with the horrible fury of the wind. It came from the roof just above Max's fitfully sleeping body on the bed across the room. She wondered if even in his drugged state of unconsciousness Max heard the Teeka trying to reach him.

It couldn't come in the house. At least it never had before. As Ida crossed the attic, her attention was riveted on Max. The flame from the lamp on the bookcase at the foot of Joey and Max's beds fluttered as a draft made its way into the room.

Ida noticed that Joey was awake. He was sitting up shaking in his bed. His arms were wrapped around himself to control his shivering body against the chill that had begun to creep into the room. The blanket Ida had spread over him was now wadded at his waist. He was staring at his father, horror so deeply etched on his face that Ida felt her own blood cool.

"You should be sleeping," said Ida. Through the effects of the tea, Ida wasn't the only one to see into their thoughts and memories. They had all been linked, and Joey had seen his father's desires and his plans for them. It was no longer suspicion that his father wanted to kill him and his mother. Joey knew it. He'd seen his father's plan to trap them up here and set fire to the cabin. He'd seen the vile, evil nature of his father.

"I know," soothed Ida. "I'm truly sorry you had to see it. But now you know. Now you understand. I'm glad you're awake. Come help me." She held up the rope for Joey to see. "My hands aren't so strong anymore."

Joey nodded, unraveled himself from the blanket, and swung his legs over the edge of the bed. He swayed a bit when he stood up, but he quickly recovered. "I don't want to kill him," said Joey. "I should, but I don't."

"We're not gonna do that," said Ida. "We're just gonna tie him up so he can't kill us. You remember what you saw?"

Joey nodded. "Was that real?"

"Yes, as real as the nose on your face."

"Yeah, I thought so," he said. "I didn't know what happened to the baby. She just told me that she lost it, that it was sick."

"Now you know," said Ida. "Now you can help her heal that awful black hole in her heart. She would never have told you; she couldn't even face it herself. But now that you know, maybe that'll help her open herself up, let some light back into her soul."

Joey nodded. "I hope so. I'll try to help her."

"That's all anyone can do," replied Ida.

"What's going to happen to Dad?"

Ida couldn't tell what Joey hoped for, but she wouldn't lie to him.

"He's going away somewhere he won't ever be able to hurt you or your mother or anyone else ever again." Ida looked squarely into Joey's eyes. "Does that sit alright with you?"

"Yes, ma'am," answered Joey, with no hesitation. "Are you sure he won't come back?"

"I'm sure," she replied.

"Good," said Joey.

"Come on now," said Ida. "We need to get him tied up."

"Okay."

They tied one end of rope around Max's right hand, then laced it under the bed and tied up his left hand with the other end. Then they repeated the process with Max's feet. He snorted and snored, and a few times he mumbled something, but he never woke.

When they were done, Joey asked Ida, "Is the Teeka going to take him away?"

"Yes, honey."

"Will it kill him?"

"Honestly, honey, I don't know what it will do with him."

"Okay," said Joey. "I don't want him to ever come back, though. I never want him to hurt Mom again."

"He won't, honey. He won't."

"Um." Joey was embarrassed.

"What is it, honey?" asked Ida.

He looked down a moment before meeting Ida's eyes. "Did your sister, Eugenia, hurt you?"

Ida winced. "Yes, she did, honey. She hurt me real bad."

"I'm sorry," he said, hugging Ida. "I'm sorry about Maggie too, that you couldn't be with her."

Ida muffled a sob. "Thank you, honey."

Chapter 27

Ida convinced Joey to go back to bed. He protested, but moments after his head hit the pillow, he was soundly adrift in slumber. Ida descended the stairs, the oil lamp held up to light her way. She blew out the flame and set the lamp on the kitchen counter. Extinguishing the other lamps, Ida shuffled by flickering firelight to the fireplace. She stirred the coals and piled on the night's final three logs.

Ida didn't have the strength to change into her nightgown, so she pulled off her boots, took off her dungarees, and slipped under the covers in her socks, long underwear, and shirt. Gigi curled up beside her, as Ida drifted off to sleep.

The tea sometimes had residual effects, drawing up memories in her dreams that she would rather not see. But in this case, it wasn't the tea but her tortured soul that forced her to relive her past.

Hollow Junction consisted of a small trading post and a rustic log church. The few scattered farms squatting in the depths of the Hollows made up the rest of the loose community. Even when Ida was a little girl, the land was already winning the battle against settlement. Every year a few more people left the region for an easier life, the deep hollows having thwarted their attempts to claim it for themselves. And something dark lurked there. It had a name, which no one uttered for fear of summoning it.

The church was a low building of logs with no steeple. There was a heavy iron bell on a tall post near the dirt path that passed for a road in front of the church. The bell rang out on Sundays to call people to service and served as an emergency signal as well, its sharp clang easily reached into the hills. It was ringing now. It was not Sunday.

People arrived at the church, chores and fieldwork laid aside to respond to the call from the bell. A half-dozen people milled about speculating while their more far-flung neighbors finally rode down the hollows to the junction. The thick forest crowded in close, as if attempting to heal the wound cut through it.

The church door opened, and Pastor Everett stepped out of the rough building, followed by Joseph Grover and his wife, Margery. Joseph's face was ashen and grave, and his wife could not walk unassisted, her strength consumed by weeping.

"Folks," called Pastor Everett, raising his hands to quiet the gathered farmers and their wives, his voice strong and clear. "The devil himself has visited us this day!"

The crowd was silent.

"Dear little Clara Grover has been murdered," he announced, his voice cracking in an effort to suppress the choked sob in his throat.

The farmers erupted in anger and shock, their voices a din of outrage.

Pastor Everett yelled over their voices to share the details.

"Her mother," he placed a hand on Margery's shoulder, "found her brutalized body just two hours ago at Slater's Rock, near their farm. Clara went missing last night." He turned his eyes to the two-horse wagon pulled up next to the church, a canvas-covered body resting in its open bed.

The men pushed forward to see the nature of the crime for themselves, committed on one of their most innocent. Someone pulled the canvas back and gasps of revulsion shrilled in the air. Some covered their faces, and more than one turned to retch onto the ground. Anger quickly swelled among those gathered.

The battered, tiny body lay exposed in the back of the wagon, her mother wailing fresh shrieks of grief. Clara's slight form lay supine, her sightless eyes cast upward to the cold blue sky above, one eye swollen and bruised. Her mouth gaped open unnaturally wide, as if caught in a scream. The edges of her mouth were torn and ragged, like something rough had been forced inside. Dark bruises circled her neck, but the true horror lay in her private region. Her plain brown cotton dress, stained with dirt and blood, was hitched up, exposing her ruined genitals. The bloody mass of pulpy flesh looked as though a meat grinder had been taken to it. Her thighs were coated in dried blood and gore. The cold of early winter rendered her exposed skin a grayish blue. Smaller wounds on her legs, arms, and face suggested animals had begun to take notice of her.

Ida tried to blot out the images of what happened next. But she couldn't. She was captive in her own mind to relive the scenes. No matter how many times the dream visited her, the trauma and sorrow never lessened.

Ida sat on the buckboard of her old wagon, with Oats, her old, slope-backed horse harnessed in the traces. Ida had come to the trading post for flour and chicken scratch that morning, when the clanging bell drew her attention. Her parents had died the year before, sickness taking them both a few weeks apart, and their cabin and homestead had gone to Ida—their eldest child and caregiver in their final declining years. Her sister had married years before and moved to her husband's farm two hollows over. Her brother had married and moved away the previous spring, unwilling to sacrifice his life to the toils of the Hollows. Ida watched the men's faces as they peered into the wagon by the church. She shrank from the horror reflected on them.

This will be bad, she thought.

A late-arriving wagon lurched down the ragged road from Johnson Hollow, a narrow twisting valley of damp, spongy ground. It was her sister, Eugenia, and her husband, Evan. Weeks before, Eugenia had accused Ida of flirting with Evan, trying to lure him away from his wedding vows.

Eugenia glared at Ida across the crowd, her angular face stern and dark. Ida looked away. She thought of Maggie, whom she hadn't seen since the baby was born. She searched the faces in the crowd, but Maggie was not among them. After Maggie gave birth, people looked at Ida differently. Distrust and fear blatant in their stares. Some of the younger ones Ida herself had delivered—being the only midwife in the Hollows. Maggie's was a difficult birth, and Ida felt the shift of people's suspicions toward her afterward.

As Ida ventured another look at her sister, she was greeted by a menacing smile that blossomed quickly before slipping away. Eugenia's face hardened to a cold stare that chilled Ida's heart.

"She did this!" screamed Eugenia, her voice carrying over the crowd. Stares from their neighbors and friends turned to see who made this accusation, and whom she indicted.

Ida was struck dumb. She couldn't fathom the depths of Eugenia's betrayal.

"No, no, no," said Ida, her voice weak with fear. She shook her head adamantly.

Without pause, Ida snapped the reins, spurring Oats forward. The wagon jerked and sped in a tight circle, dust billowing from the dry dirt road. She understood Eugenia's plan. Her heart certain of the ramifications to follow. Her sister meant to put an end to Ida. To condemn her for all her perceived guilt, and the secret she kept.

Ida's heart pounded. "No! It's not true!" she screamed, her eyes pleading to the neighbors she'd known her entire life.

"She stole poor Clara's soul to pay back the devil!" Shouted Eugenia. It landed as gospel with many.

"She tried to do the same to me when I was a little girl! And she tried to steal my husband with her magic!" screamed Eugenia. "She has lain with the devil, and women, against God's word!"

Oats had slowed to a nervous walk as someone grabbed at the harnesses. Others crowded toward the wagon to stop it from slipping away. The heat of the crowd's anger rose. Oats, a placid animal, spooked as angry men bumped and jostled him in their attempt to get closer.

"She made me charms for the fever last spring!" a woman, Mrs. Geller, yelled from the crowd.

"Yes! And she called the spirits down to make our soil more fertile!" called out Mrs. Greene, the woman Ida had instructed on how to grow her corn taller. They were her friends, all of them, when they needed her help, but witnesses for her accuser now.

Superstition walked hand in hand with life in the deep hollows, and Pastor Everett wasn't immune to it, either. Margery Grover, the murdered girl's mother, tugged at his arm and spoke. "Clara went to Ida last week to fetch me a remedy of herbs for a rash. We paid her with a chicken, and now she's stolen my baby away to pay the devil her debt!" Her shriek of despair sent shivers down Ida's spine.

With the certainty of the righteous, Pastor Everett waved his hands high and shouted, "Take her!"

It was all the crowd needed. All reservations dissolved, and they surged forward toward the wagon as one entity.

Ida responded by instinct alone. Had she stopped to think, they would have hauled her from the wagon then and there. But she snapped the reins hard, shouting "HAH!" at her frightened horse. Oats responded. Ida lurched backward, barely able to keep her seat on the bench as the wagon surged forward. Oats dashed ahead, clearing a path through the gathered men.

"Grab her!" A dozen hands clawed at Ida, clutching at her arms and legs, but the motion of the wagon parted them like a ship through the sea. Ida quickly found herself beyond them, barreling up the trail that led to her home two miles distant.

She knew they'd come after her, that she must quickly figure out what to do. Her mind raced as fast as the wagon she was driving, grasping for something to stave off the coming horror. The good Christians of the Hollows did not tolerate witchcraft. Ida, always aware, walked a fine line following the ways of her grandmother. She'd taught Ida everything she knew about the plants and trees and animals of these mountains, supplemented by Ida's own considerable natural abilities. But fear supplanted rational thought in her mind, and all she could think to do was get home before the angry mob caught up to her.

As she slept, Ida's body twitched and lunged under her covers, sending Gigi to find a calmer place to rest. Ida moaned in her sleep, as she hurled through her past yet again.

Ida arrived home to the safety of her cabin. She scrambled from the wagon, pausing only to unhitch Oats, setting him loose to wander, and then she raced to the cabin porch. She threw open the front door and dashed inside, slamming it closed and locking it behind her.

She expected the mob to be hot on her tail, hell-bent on catching the witch to make her pay. But the road was still and empty. She wasn't foolhardy enough to believe they wouldn't be coming soon. *Just gettin' up their nerve,* she'd thought.

She hurried to the window to peer out and drew back the loosely woven curtains. But nothing stirred except poor old Oats, his head low, lips grazing the dead grass at the edge of the dirt in front of the cabin.

Ida prepared herself after Maggie gave birth to her baby girl. She knew she'd made a mistake. But she couldn't have stopped herself if she'd tried. Maggie owned Ida's heart. She would not let Maggie and her baby end that way. And so, calling on the old knowledge Ida's grandmother had taught her, she'd used the old recipe to bring them back. Her grandmother had been reluctant to teach her how and said people would call it the devil's work. And maybe it was, but there weren't any whispered words or spells, just carefully measured herbs, some known more as poison than medicine, and some fungus distillates she'd made in her kitchen and kept packed in her bag. And they'd worked!

Maggie's husband had seen Maggie and their child as they lay dead and then afterward, as the spark of life returned to them both. She'd seen the stark terror in his eyes. Looking at his face, Ida realized she'd gone too far—that he believed this had not been the result of carefully prepared ingredients, but from the devil himself. And she knew then that she was marked. That was when she began her preparations, all the while hoping they would never become necessary.

As the gray gloom of morning blanketed the hollow, panic seized Ida as riders gathered on the road near her cabin, the breath of their horses fogged in the frigid air. Pastor Everett reined in his horse just a few feet from the cabin porch.

"Ida Wheeling!" he called out, hard and strong—the voice in church each week banished evil from the hearts and minds of his flock.

Ida's tears streaked her cheeks as she watched. How could they believe this of her? But she knew the sight of Clara Grover's violated body had dispelled reason from their minds. There was no thought, only reaction. They wanted someone to hold accountable for the terrible crime committed. But they had it wrong. It hadn't been Ida who'd killed the little girl. Ida, who cringed when she killed a chicken for her stewpot, wasn't capable of those horrible acts.

"I didn't do that to her, Pastor. I couldn't do that!" Her voice broke into sobs, as she shouted through the window.

"You've been accused! We all know what you do here!" He wouldn't listen to reason. He couldn't hear it. He could hear only the imagined screams of pain and terror of a little girl. He was as blinded as the rest of them. His mind refused to see beyond the horror in his heart.

"It's just folk craft. Anyone could do it! It's just mixin' plants to heal a wound! The Devil never crossed my threshold! I'd not have him here!" But she knew it was done. In the bleak morning light of the bitterly cold day, she saw the men dismount and move toward her cabin.

"Come out, Ida! Come out and be tried! You'll get your chance to speak your truth!"

But Ida knew that was a lie. She knew it because the other men spread out around her cabin. They were making sure she couldn't escape. She was trapped. Some of the men carried torches of sticks and torn strips of canvas wrapped around the tips. They carried them high on display for her to see, like banners to condemn her.

She closed her eyes and shook her head slowly. *Lord don't let this happen. Please!* Her pleas were useless. She opened her eyes and saw the lit torches. Panic stampeded through her heart.

"Please!" she called out. "This is wrong! There's no proof!" Her fear and frustration threatened to overwhelm her. She stepped away from the window, knowing there was only one choice left to her. Her eyes scoured every corner of the cabin for some avenue to halt this injustice. But it was pointless. With resignation, her eyes fell to the carefully prepared mug sitting on the countertop, a heavy cloth draped over it.

A gasp escaped her lips. Her grandmother had drilled into Ida's head ceaselessly, *always praise the Lord, and never draw attention when you practice the healing art.* And Ida had heeded those words as best she could. But to no avail—the very people she'd helped, now held her in suspicion and fear.

Eugenia's face flashed into Ida's mind. Eugenia always envied Ida's easy manner and the fact that people genuinely liked her, though that seemed a falsehood now. But she never thought Eugenia would bear blatantly false witness against her. *It was guilt*, she thought, and knew it was true.

Eugenia had reluctantly visited Ida the previous spring, strangely humble. She needed a remedy. She was pregnant and needed to be rid of the tiny life growing inside her. She wouldn't say why.

Days later, Ida had seen Eugenia at the trading post. She'd seen the looks pass between her sister and the stranger who'd arrived the winter before and worked there. He was a handsome man with strapping muscles and fiery red hair—Ida just knew that he was the father, not Eugenia's husband, Evan. And Ida was the only one who knew, besides Eugenia.

Ida hurried to the kitchen. The water in the kettle was not yet hot, but it was warm. *It'll have to do,* she thought. She was out of time.

She barely registered Pastor Everett's voice as he called out once more.

"Ida Wheeling, come out now, or you'll be judged guilty!"

She knew she'd already been judged guilty in their hearts, and to surrender now would only hasten the inevitable. She ignored Pastor Everett and finished mixing the herbs and water in the cup.

She took up a bundle of cloth from the counter. Tied inside were dried ground roots, and herbs to call the Teeka—herbs that never grew together, some from the dry ridge top, others from the lush and swampy valley floor. She stirred the glowing coals in the fireplace and nestled the bundled cloth on top. Flames quickly flared at the edges of the cloth and enveloped the bundle in a flash of crimson.

"The poison is only poison if you don't know how to use it," whispered Ida, repeating her grandmother's words, not as an incantation but as affirmation.

A new sound met her ears. The commotion of jittery horses and the shouts of men, mingled now with a crackling, rushing sound that Ida recognized at once. They'd set fire to the cabin. They were going to smoke her out or burn her alive.

From the charred bundle of herbs in the fireplace, a noxious, putrid-green smoke billowed up the chimney. When only fading embers remained, Ida took up the mug from the table and lifted it to her lips. She spied smoke leaking through the joints of the wall logs, curling up toward the ceiling. Stifling a cry, she choked down the entire contents of the mug, registering the darkly bitter flavor coating her throat with a disgusted gasp. Fire rushed up outside the windows, and the light in the cabin flared bright and accusatory. The heat through the window caused the curtains to smoke and then burst into flames. The smoke was thick and harsh. Flames seeped through the cracked chinking between the logs.

Ida felt the effects of the tea almost immediately. Her throat seized, choking off her breath, her heart raced in her chest, reminding her of the furious pounding of Oats' hooves on the harried race home the day before. Her ruddy face turned bluish-purple, and she staggered and dropped into the chair by the fireplace.

She couldn't see the smoke now. Her sight had been stolen—her eyes gone blind. Somewhere above her, outside the cabin, she heard a great gusting wind, like a tornado splitting the world, and shouts of terror from the men gathered outside. The horses shrieked in fear, and their thudding hoofs thundered as they raced away from whatever horror had descended from the sky. Suddenly dizzy, Ida's body seized with sickness. A billion pricks needled her skin, dissolving her essence. Finally, after agonizing moments, Ida felt nothing at all.

Chapter 28

Ida woke with a start. The cabin shuddered against the wind's assault. The fire in the hearth was low, and heavy shadows loomed around her. The air wasn't cold, but the cabin had lost its coziness. The fire would need tending soon. With each blast of wind, threads of frigid air streamed in through tiny fissures between the logs next to her bed. Outside the temperature was dropping. The snow was easing off, and bitter cold was moving in behind it.

Ida noticed Gigi curled up on the pillow next to her. "Good morning, Gigi," she said quietly. "Busy day today."

Soft predawn light washed the room with a sepia quality. Grunting, Ida threw off the blankets. She shivered, goosebumps rising on her skin as she struggled to stand up. She drew on her dungarees, hooking the straps over her shoulders, and slipped her feet into her rabbit-fur slippers. There were chores to do.

Above, the attic was quiet. Ida's slippers scuffed like sandpaper against the floorboards as she shuffled to the fireplace. She stirred the coals and stacked fresh logs onto the grate. The pale blue gauze of light creeping in through the window above the cook-stove told Ida that sunrise was still an hour away.

She took the spill down from the mantel and held the tip in the growing flames until it caught. Shielding the tiny flame with one hand, she carried it over to the lamp in the kitchen, lifted the glass chimney, and touched the flame to the blackened wick. The flame caught immediately, sputtering lightly before flaring full and bright. She blew out the spill and fitted the chimney back into place, adjusting the flame slightly. The soft lamplight was a gentle, soothing fairytale glow that took her back to her childhood. Though its shine couldn't reach the farthest corners of the cabin, it was enough for her to set about her work.

Ida hoped that this would be the last time she would have to repeat these trials. She was weary of her eternal winter. Even as the steel gray day grew brighter, the air grew colder. She dreamed of spring and the fresh scent of warmed earth. Oh, how she missed it.

Ida rekindled a fire in the cook-stove. She ladled water into the copper kettle from the half-full pail on the floor and set it on the stovetop to heat.

Sighing, she felt pressure in her bladder. Kicking off her slippers and nudging them under her bed, Ida pulled on her boots; the old leather was creased and rough, but comfortable.

Slipping on her coat and setting her wide-brimmed leather hat snuggly on her head, Ida looked up when she heard one of the beds upstairs creaking.

Worst part coming soon, she thought. Bracing against the cold, she opened the front door and stepped out into the brutal wind and swirling snow of the frigid gray morning.

It had stopped snowing, but the incessant wind had sculpted drifts three and four feet high. Ida felt the ice stinging her legs, like icy tongues. She trampled her way to the outhouse. Inside, she shucked her pants down to her knees and sat down on the frozen wooden bench. "Oh mercy!" she exclaimed, at the bitter cold wood against her skin. She closed her eyes and breathed deeply as her bladder emptied.

As Ida left the outhouse, she heard Sugar bellowing *MOOO!* She also heard Oats' impatiently stomping his hooves.

"I'll get there soon!" she called out. Normally, the animals would be tended first, but today there was a more pressing agenda inside the cabin.

Ida climbed the steps and pushed open the door of the cabin. Inside, she heard an angry voice hollering from the attic. *I guess Max is awake.* She shouted up the stairs, "Hold your horses! You ain't the only animal needs tendin' to!"

Chapter 29

"What in the world!" shrieked Rhonda.

"Untie me, you fucking bitch!"

Ida dashed as quickly as she could to the base of the stairs and shouted up to Rhonda. "Honey! Come on down here, please. We need to talk."

Rhonda didn't answer. Ida heard Max struggling to free himself from the bed, the wooden frame protesting with tortured squeaks at his violent movements.

Rhonda appeared at the top of the stairs. Joey was right behind her, looking sheepish, guilty for his part in restraining his father.

"Ida? What's going on?" Rhonda's eyes darted from Ida to her husband tied to the bed across the room. Rhonda had to know what was happening. She'd seen her husband's thoughts and plans along with the rest of them.

"Come along," coaxed Ida. "Get your boots and come down."

"What the fuck do you think you're doing!" Max's scream reverberated through the cabin. "Let me the fuck loose!"

Rhonda retrieved her boots and made her way down the steep stairs. Joey followed behind her.

"Joey! Get your fucking faggot ass back here!" screamed Max. But neither Joey nor Rhonda heeded him, infuriating Max even more. "I'm going to fucking kill you all!"

"Yes," Ida called out. "That's why you're tied up."

Rhonda and Joey joined Ida near the fireplace. "Your face looks better today," said Ida, examining the cut and swelling on Joey's cheek.

"Yes, ma'am," replied Joey, lightly touching his face.

"Fuck you, old lady!" yelled Max. There was a pause, and then Max screeched, "Oh my God! Christ, I'm going to shit the fucking bed!"

Ida winced at Joey. "I'm gonna need your help."

"No, he can't go back up there," insisted Rhonda.

"Well," said Ida, "I'd just as soon not go up there either, but I'd like it less if I had to clean him up *after* he soiled hisself and the bed."

Rhonda couldn't argue. "Be careful," she said.

Ida took the shotgun down from its pegs and carried it to the kitchen.

"I'm not kidding!" yelled Max, a piercing plea.

Ida ignored him. She set the gun on the counter and opened the cabinet below it. Withdrawing a squat ceramic pot with a wide opening and rounded lip, she handed it to Joey. Then she took out a roll of toilet paper and a few cloth rags. She regarded them for a moment before putting the toilet paper back into the cabinet and closing the door. "That's the last roll," she said. "Rags should do fine."

Joey nodded, realizing what they were about to do.

"Honey," Ida said to Rhonda, "Would you go out to the cold box on the porch and bring in the slab of bacon, please? It's wrapped up tight in burlap, can't miss it." She smiled, picked up the shotgun again, and started for the stairs.

Rhonda watched them go, then went out onto the front porch to get the bacon. The wind was howling down the hollow. Shivering from the cold, Rhonda brought the bacon in from the snow-covered storage box and set it down on the countertop. Her heart felt like lead in her chest as she recalled the moment Max had terminated her pregnancy. Rhonda flushed with humiliation upon realizing the others had shared the memory with her.

In the attic, Ida stood at the foot of Max's bed. Joey had been a real trooper following her directions and partially releasing Max from his bonds so he could relieve himself, and then retying his father to the bed. Afterward, she'd sent Joey back downstairs with the sloshing chamber pot. *The act of living could be such a messy business, sometimes.*

Max, for his part, had followed Ida's directions exactly—not much choice with a shotgun pointed at his head—though his eyes seethed with rage the whole time.

"You know," Max said. "Dreams don't mean anything. Dreams aren't actions. I haven't done anything to deserve this." He raised his arms, fists tightly clenched, and peered at the ropes tied to his wrists as if he were Christ on the cross.

"You murdered your unborn child, near fully formed in the womb!" spat Ida. "And you planned on killing your family and me too, for good measure. It's right there in your eyes even if I hadn't seen it play out from your mind."

Max didn't react. He didn't even try to argue the point. His muscles were taut, ready to strike if the chance presented itself. He didn't try to hide it. It wasn't a secret. "So, what now?" he asked, his face a blank slate.

"I'm gonna go down and fix breakfast for everyone, even you," replied Ida.

Max struggled, but Ida's finger hadn't once left the trigger of the gun. He didn't doubt for a second, she wouldn't hesitate to pull that trigger.

Ida studied Max's face. "You got a twinkle in your eyes you're tryin' to hide."

Max kept his face calm, only deigning to turn his head and glance at her innocently.

"No matter," said Ida. "Whatever you're thinkin', it ain't gonna do you no good. I've been around a long time. Pretty sure I've seen most of the tricks. Someone will bring up some food in a bit."

"Wonderful," said Max. "I've got to keep up my strength."

Ida ignored him and started down the stairs.

A devilish smile crept onto Max's face as he watched Ida descend the stairs. He had a secret that was about to change the rules in this little game. When he had laid back down on the bed and Joey scurried around to retie his wrists, Max had noticed a small lump under his left hip. As Ida had prattled on, a sudden flash of memory from the night before flared in Max's mind.

His anger had been palpable, but with Ida's tea swirling through his head there was nothing he could do with it. Max had done the only thing he could to calm himself. He'd reached into his pocket and drew out his pocketknife. Such a small thing, but it imparted an almost euphoric peace to his soul. He'd clutched it in his hand like a talisman until he'd drifted off. He realized now he must have dropped it after he fell asleep, and it'd rested hidden in the folds of the sheet since then.

Now, all he had to do was maneuver his arms to allow enough slack in the rope, and he could reach the knife. The rope was strung under the bed and up on each side where the ends were tied to his wrists. When he dropped his right arm toward the floor, it allowed enough slack for his left hand to explore the wadded folds of the sheet. His humiliation from the last half hour fueled his resolve. The wicked grin slipped from his lips, and was replaced by a puckered grim line of satisfaction.

Chapter 30

"I'll take that to the outhouse," offered Rhonda, nodding with mild disgust at Max's chamber pot that Joey had set on the floor near the front door. "I've really got to go," she said, pulling on her coat.

"Thank you, honey," replied Ida. "I'll get breakfast started." She finished pouring water over Joey's hands to rinse off the lye soap into the washtub, and then handed him a dishtowel to dry them. To Joey, she said, "Honey, would you mind shoveling the path to the barn again? I'm afraid the wind covered it over last night."

Joey was only too happy to get out of the cabin. His mind was still reeling from the revelations of the night before, and then the incredible sight of his captive father this morning.

"Yes, ma'am," he replied. Then he added, "I can feed and water Sugar and Oats too. If you want me to."

"That'd be real nice," Ida said. "Thank you."

"Should I shovel to the chicken coop too?" He got his coat down from the peg and pulled it on as his mother picked up the chamber pot from the floor.

"Yes, please," said Ida, absently. She was busying herself at the cookstove now, stoking up the fire again and retrieving her cast iron skillet from its hook. "Water them too, if you would. There's a sack of scratch in the barn. Toss a scoop in the bowl in the coop." She thought for a second then added, "If you're a mind to, you can check the nestin' boxes for eggs. Don't take no bunk from the hens neither."

Joey smiled. "No, ma'am, I won't."

"Be sure to close the barn door behind you. You can leave that window near Sugar's stall open. Wind's comin' from the other side, and they'll appreciate the light."

Rhonda stood holding the foul-smelling chamber pot, waiting for Joey to finish zipping up his coat so he could open the door for her.

"Sorry, mom." Joey quickly reached past her to open the door. The wind whipped into the cabin with tremendous force. Joey's vision of happily shoveling the path and tending to the animals was quickly dispelled as he realized how strong the wind was blowing. And just how cold he was going to be. But he'd said he would do it so there was nothing to be done but work through it as quickly as he could.

Following his mother out the door, Joey struggled to pull it closed.

Ida unwrapped the bacon. With her razor-sharp knife she deftly cut the thawing slab into slices and lay them out in the hot skillet. The bacon sizzled and popped, and Ida hummed her little song all the while listening for sounds from the attic above.

"Everything alright up there?" she called out, shooting a look up the stairs.

There was a muffled squeak from Max's bed, and his vitriolic reply bellowed out. "Fuck you, bitch!"

Ida smiled. "Such a foul mouth on that one," she mumbled. She knew he was plotting something. "Won't matter," she said, using a fork to turn the bacon.

Something niggled at the back of Joey's mind. He tried to bring it to the forefront, but it wouldn't budge. His mom was in a hurry to get to the outhouse, so she went ahead of him carrying the chamber pot along the trail Ida had left earlier. The wind had begun to erase the path again, but it was still passable.

Joey tugged the shovel out of the snow that had accumulated on the porch, the wind trying to rip it from his hands. The morning sky was overcast, dull, and gray. Although the snow had stopped, the wind now took up the mantle, scouring the powder from the ground and hurling it through the air. The outhouse could barely be seen through the shifting veils of white.

With his hood cinched tight around his face and his gloves snug on his hands, every gust of wind still sucked the heat from his body. He did his best to ignore the cold. He could hear Sugar mooing over the roar of another approaching torrent of wind.

As he made his way beyond his mother's tracks and began to shovel the path toward the barn, the outhouse door banged open behind him. The adrenaline jolt ripped through Joey's body. He lunged forward and struggled to keep from pitching over into the snow, like a staggering drunk.

Joey swiveled around. His mother emerged from the outhouse, carrying the empty chamber pot. She looked at Joey apologetically, realizing she had startled him.

"Sorry!" she called.

Joey could barely hear her over the wind. He smiled and waved. Niggle, niggle. Something to do with his father.

He watched his mother close the door. Then she approached Joey, her arms out like a tightrope walker to keep from slipping. "Are you okay? Do you need help?"

Her face looked bleak and tired. Her mouth was drawn tight, the lines around it prominent. Her eyes looked lost, the world no longer a place she recognized.

Joey hated seeing her this way. Shaking his head, he said, "No thanks, Mom. I can handle it."

Rhonda smiled. "I love you, Joey." She leaned forward and kissed him on the cheek.

"I love you, too."

"If you get too cold, you be sure to stop and come back to the cabin. The animals can wait if you need to warm up."

"I will," said Joey. He wanted to mention what was troubling him. But since he couldn't quite figure out what it was it seemed useless to bring it up. He smiled and turned back to shoveling.

Rhonda smiled tenderly and made her way back to the cabin. She picked up the chamber pot along the way.

Joey finally reached the barn, sweat trickling down his forehead. Sugar sounded distressed. He opened the door and stepped inside, momentarily blind in the dim shadows of the barn's interior.

"I'm coming, Sugar," soothed Joey. His words seemed to calm the large animal. He hurried across the barn and unlatched the window closest to her stall. He pulled it open, and a shaft of light pierced the darkness.

Niggle.

For crying out loud! What am I forgetting?

He threw back the latch and yanked open the stall door. He stepped back as Sugar surged out. She snorted as she buried her nose in his coat, inhaling his scent.

"You're okay now," Joey said, rubbing her coarse forehead. He picked up the splitting maul and carried it into the stall. He jammed it down into the water trough. The ice shattered, but it took several strikes before he broke through to the water below. There wasn't much left unfrozen. He spied a water bucket just outside the stall. He sighed when he realized he'd have to shovel a path to the creek gurgling along behind the barn, too.

He carried the ice chunks to the window and pitched them out into the snow. By the time he was done, his hands were stiff with cold. He rubbed them together furiously and stopped to flex them from time to time, trying to work the circulation back into them.

After cleaning and freshening Sugar's stall, Joey tried to coax the cow back inside, but she was having none of it. He copied the clicking sound he'd heard Ida use the evening before to entice the animal. Nothing. She just stood in the middle of the barn mooing belligerently at Joey.

"Come on, Sugar," he pleaded.

Just then he heard footsteps out in the snow. His heart froze in terror.

He managed to breathe again when the door opened, and Ida made her way inside.

"She's got to be milked," said Ida. "Don't know how I forgot about that." She picked up a small three-legged stool and a metal pail from the corner of the barn. Joey hadn't even noticed them before.

At the sight of Ida carrying the stool and pail, Sugar mooed loudly again and walked back into her stall.

"Has to be done every evening and every morning," explained Ida as she set the stool on the ground next to Sugar's side. Then she slowly lowered herself onto the stool and set the pail under Sugar's bulging udder.

"It gets full and makes her fierce uncomfortable."

Ida reached under the cow. She started to work Sugar's teats, squeezing and pulling on them in a practiced motion. Joey was amazed as streams of steaming milk squirted into the pail.

"There isn't much water left in the trough," said Joey. "I'll shovel over to the creek and get some more."

"Thank you, Joey. I sure do appreciate your help," said Ida, as her hands continued their steady rhythm.

"You're welcome, ma'am. Thank you for taking us in," said Joey, a small lump formed in his throat.

Ida chuckled. "I guess I'm not gonna get you to call me Ida, am I?"

"Sorry, ma'...Ida," said Joey. He took the empty water bucket and headed out to shovel a path to the creek.

His mind persisted.

Niggle.

The sweet, fatty smell of frying bacon wafted up the stairs from the kitchen and elicited a loud grumble from Max's stomach. He was starving. But more than that, he was angry and focused like a laser on his task.

He'd managed to get the knife open, but the angle was difficult for him to cut the rope. First, he thought he might be able to use the tip of the blade to work loose the knot around his wrist. But he found it impossible to apply enough pressure to wiggle the blade between the loops of rope. But he did find he was able to bear down hard enough with short, slow strokes, drawing the blade back and forth across the twisted cordage. The going was infuriatingly slow. But he could see a small cleft in the rope beginning to form as the blade began to separate the fibers.

Take your time. Do it right. Don't drop the fucking knife, he coached himself over and over.

The smell of cooking food, though, was a distraction that he was finding hard to ignore.

Focus.

His grumbling stomach rippled through his entire body. The blade slipped.

Fuck!

The knife slipped off the rope and almost tumbled to the floor.

Lying back, he relaxed his arm, the knife now safely cupped in his hand again. He let his muscles rest for a few minutes before repositioning the knife. Resuming his efforts, he made slow, steady progress.

Rhonda stood at the stove. She'd never cooked with wood before. In the case of frying bacon, there wasn't much finesse involved. The stove was hot. It heated the cast iron pan. The bacon cooked. If it started to cook too fast, Ida told her to slide the pan over a little, so it wasn't directly over the flames in the firebox. But she couldn't imagine baking something like the delicious bread Ida had made the previous evening.

Ida had forgotten to milk Sugar, the cow, and had asked Rhonda to take over cooking the bacon. Then she'd grabbed her coat and disappeared out the door.

Now Rhonda could see Joey outside shoveling a path to the creek, then hauling buckets of water back to the barn.

Rhonda knew what Max had been planning to do to them. She'd literally seen it. They all had. She also understood that something was going to have to be done about it. She strongly suspected Ida already had her own ideas about that, but Rhonda found herself trying to push the whole business out of her mind.

The way you always do.

The thought stung. It was all so painful to think about, especially her own pitiful shortcomings. She chastised herself for her inability to leave Max years ago, the way any sane person would have. And yet here they were. She'd spent the better part of the last ten years pushing the unpleasantness—her euphemism for beatings—as far away as she could manage.

Rhonda heard a squeaking upstairs. Her mind flashed a vision of Max lunging at her down the stairs, blind fury blazing from his eyes, his fists raised to beat her to death. But there was no one there.

Joey finished digging out the path to the creek. He managed to dip the bucket into the rushing water and pull it out again, without slipping down the icy bank. He could imagine how cold it would be if he'd slipped. Dangerously cold. He dumped a few inches of water out of the bucket to keep it from sloshing down his leg as he walked back to the barn.

As he entered, he saw Ida had finished with the milking—the pail of steaming, silky white milk was set just outside of the stall. Sugar munched contentedly on the hay in the slatted feeder. Ida was now mucking out Oats' stall.

Joey poured the water into the trough and headed back out to get more.

When he returned, Ida was scattering straw in the horse's stall.

"Good boy," Joey said softly as he edged by Oats, who was standing calmly watching Ida. Joey tilted the bucket over the water trough.

"Save some for the chickens," advised Ida.

Joey pulled up short. "Okay," he said, saving about a third of the water in the bucket.

"I'll head back to the cabin with the milk," said Ida, taking up the half-full pail. "You did a real good job," she said.

"Thank you," said Joey, beaming.

"You know," said Ida, her eyes softening. "You're a real good boy, Joey. Don't you ever take anythin' to heart your daddy did or said to you.

If you was my boy, I'd be as proud of you as the sun at daybreak. Just thought you should know that."

A teary-eyed Joey hugged Ida. "Thank you."

"You're welcome." Ida nodded at a burlap sack on a shelf near the door. "Chicken scratch is in that sack. There's a can in the bag. One can full in the food dish should be fine."

"Okay, Ida," replied Joey.

Ida smiled at his use of her name, finally. "Bring in any eggs you find," she said and disappeared out into the white world.

Joey stroked Oats gently on the forehead before shooing him into the stall and closing the gate. "We'll check on you later."

Sugar watched him leave, then went back to chewing her cud.

Joey left the bucket by the barn door. He took up the shovel again and cleared a path to the chicken coop, the snow-laden wind burning his face, like tiny bee stings. He knew he should stop and go warm up in the cabin for a little while, but he decided he'd rather finish this chore and not have to come back out again until evening.

Glancing at the cabin, Joey watched Ida struggling with the milk pail as she rounded the path to the front porch. Then she disappeared from his sight. He felt a stab of guilt. He should have carried it for her.

Niggle.

Joey reached the chicken coop door. Hustling back to the barn to retrieve the water bucket, he noticed a light skim of ice already forming on the surface. He ducked inside the barn and took down the feed sack from the shelf. He scooped out a can-full and then carried it and the water bucket back to the chicken coop.

Stepping inside sent the two dozen birds into a frantic flurry of excited activity, their flapping wings stirring up clouds of dust and dander. Harried cackles pierced the air.

Coughing, Joey pulled the door closed behind him.

At last! Max grinned. He'd cut through the last few strands of rope, his left hand now free. He folded up the knife so as not to cut himself with it, then he untied his right hand and then his feet. Working stealthily, he took great care to keep the squeaks from the bed to a minimum.

The front door burst open. Ida carried in the milk pail and shoved the door closed with her foot.

"Oh, here, let me help you with that!" Rhonda hurried over from the stove. She'd taken the last of the bacon out of the pan and draped the fried strips on a plate Ida had set out.

"Thank you, honey," said Ida.

They both heard squeaks coming from upstairs. They waited, breathless, but there was nothing more.

"Expect he's getting sore, not being able to shift hisself," said Ida. "Bacon all done?"

"Yes!" said Rhonda. "I've never cooked on a wood cook-stove before."

Ida smiled. "Well, good. Let's get that milk poured into jars so it can separate; the cream floats to the top," she said with a wink.

Rhonda hauled the pail to the kitchen counter.

"Thank you, honey." Ida peered out the window at the barn and chicken coop. She saw that Joey had finished the path, and the shovel stood jammed in a mound of snow outside the chicken coop door. No sign of Joey, though.

"We'll fry up the eggs when Joey gets back," said Ida, taking three large, empty canning jars down from the shelves.

A loud thud and heavy footsteps echoed from the attic above them. Ida shot a look to the stairs and then over to the shotgun resting on its pegs by the front door.

Joey filled the feed bowl with scratch, a mix of cracked corn, and other grains. Then he poured a little water into the water dish, swirling it around. Opening the door a crack, he tossed the dirty water out.

Closing the door, he set the dish back in place and filled it to the brim. Grimy light filtered into the coop from a tiny glass window set in the opposite wall. Scurrying around the bowl, the chickens fought for position at the water dish, dipping their beaks into the cold water and then raising them into the air, like howling wolves, to swallow.

While the chickens were distracted, Joey hurried over to the nesting boxes and collected seven eggs.

Niggle.

What the hell?

It was driving him crazy. He knew it had something to do with his father. He pictured him standing outside their house, something to do with his hands. And...and he couldn't remember—too many other worries vied for his attention.

Joey set the eggs in the empty water bucket, picked up the feed can and left the chickens to their day.

Tucking the can back into the feed sack in the barn, Joey checked that Sugar and Oats still had ice-free water. Then he latched the barn door and grabbed the shovel. Careful not to rock the bucket with the eggs too much, he started the walk back to the cabin.

Just a few feet away from the barn the revelation flooded over him like Niagara Falls.

HIS KNIFE!

"He has a knife!" screamed Joey. He ran, dropping the shovel and the bucket of eggs into the deep snow beside the trail. As he passed the outhouse, Joey skidded to a stop as his mother screamed and a shotgun blast roared from inside the cabin.

Chapter 31

Joey scrambled up the steps to the front door of the cabin. He paused before opening the door. He could hear running and loud thuds thundering inside. He heard his father screaming, though he couldn't make out the words, just the angry tone. His voice sounded distant like it was coming from upstairs. Ida's voice was stern. But again, Joey couldn't hear what was said. He didn't hear his mother's voice at all. Taking a few deep breaths, Joey opened the door and peered into the cabin.

The first thing he noticed as he slinked inside was the overpowering stench of burned gunpowder. The acrid smell hung heavy in the room along with a light haze drifting on the air. The second thing he noticed was Ida standing at the base of the stairs, the shotgun held steady against her shoulder, the barrel pointed up to the attic. There were buckshot holes bored into the wall logs next to the stairs, and the uppermost step had been partially shredded by the shot.

"Joey!" shrieked Rhonda, rushing from the kitchen where she'd been cowering.

"What happened?" stammered Joey. He could hear his father moving around above them.

"He got loose," answered Ida, speaking over her shoulder, but not taking her eyes off the stairs.

"He has a knife," said Joey, guilt coloring his already rosy cheeks. "It kept nagging at me, but I couldn't remember what it was until just before I heard the shot. He keeps it in his pocket."

"Oh, sweetheart, it's not your fault." Rhonda reassured Joey before pulling him into a tight hug. "I'd forgotten about it too."

"No matter," said Ida. "We'll need to block the stairs. Keep him from gettin' down here."

"Did you shoot him?" asked Joey. He wasn't sure if he hoped she had or not.

"No," said Ida. "Scared him real good, though!"

Joey smiled. "What can we use to block the stairs?"

Ignoring Joey's question, Ida changed the subject. "Chickens alright?"

"Yes. I dropped the eggs, though, when I heard the shot."

"Break 'em?" asked Ida.

"I don't know. They were in the water bucket. The snow is soft, though. Maybe some are okay. I can go check."

"That'd be real nice," said Ida. "Eggs and bacon gonna be breakfast. Just bring the bucket in. If they're broke, we can still scramble 'em up." Her eyes twinkled at Joey.

Heading back outside, Joey heard a quiet "Psst" from Ida.

He turned around. Ida was motioning with her head for him to approach. He quietly hurried over.

Ida whispered into Joey's ear. "Can you get up the stairs and grab that rope handle on the hatch?" She looked up the stairs, and Joey followed her eyes.

He was amazed he hadn't noticed it before. There was a hinged hatch at the top of the stairs. Opened, as it was now, it leaned against the log wall to give access to the attic. The rope handle was knotted through a hole in the upper edge of the hatch and hung down a foot or so. If he could get it closed, they could tie the handle to something and keep his father trapped up there.

Joey nodded. He slowly inched his way up the first few steps, careful not to make any noise.

Rhonda held her breath until Joey reached the seventh step and was about to grab the rope handle.

"Oh no, you don't!" yelled Max, appearing at the edge of the opening, his hand shot out to grab Joey's arm. He'd been lurking just out of sight, hoping for a chance like this. He wasn't averse to using his son as a hostage to bargain his way out of this. Maybe a few solid punches to his son's face, and they'd know he meant business.

Joey was his father's son. He'd spent his life second-guessing his father's reaction to everything he did to mitigate the severity of his father's punishments. As Joey inched his way up the stairs, he'd bet that his father was hiding there, just waiting for someone to try something like this.

His timing was exquisite. As he neared the rope handle, the anticipation became dizzying. But he held off just long enough to get a little bit closer. Even as Max was yelling and lunging at Joey, Joey had already launched himself at the rope, grabbed it tightly, and simply dropped himself down the stairs, like a sandbag. Max's hands fumbled but never made contact with Joey. Joey slid down the stairs, thudding painfully on his side, but didn't release the rope.

As the hatch pulled shut, Max yelped as the rough wooden edge scraped painfully across his outstretched arm before he could lurch back out of the way. "Motherfucker!" he screamed in surprise.

The heavy oak hatch slammed shut with a puff of displaced dust and a bang as loud as the shotgun blast. Dishes in the washbasin rattled from the vibration. Joey held onto the rope to keep the hatch closed. Max was trying furiously to yank it open again.

"Slide the bolt!" hollered Ida.

Joey lurched up and down like a marionette as his father pulled on the other end of the rope handle.

Joey clung to the rope with both hands. He hadn't even noticed the heavy iron slide-bolt hidden between the ends of the ceiling rafters until Ida shouted. While gripping the rope with one hand, he reached up with the other and pulled the slide-bolt toward him. The thick end of the bolt slid into the hole in the edge of the hatch, locking it tight. Joey let go of the rope as his father continued to pull at it. The iron latch rattled against its guide, but otherwise it didn't budge.

"Oh, thank God!" Rhonda rushed to Joey as he came down the stairs and hugged him.

Joey's heart pounded.

Ida grinned. "Now, how 'bout them eggs?"

"I'll fucking kill every one of you motherfuckers!" screamed Max, his voice muffled by the heavy wooden hatch.

Ida glanced up at the stairs but didn't respond. She carried the shotgun over to its pegs and put it away.

"I'll get the eggs," said Joey. He opened the door and hurried out into the wind again.

"I'm grateful," said Rhonda, "But Joey could have been badly hurt. Max could have killed him." She teared up.

Ida held Rhonda's hand. "He could have killed all of us. Joey's a brave boy." She opened the firebox door and stoked the flames.

Rhonda sank into a chair. "What happens now?"

"That's somethin' we're gonna have to talk about. But we should eat first. Decisions shouldn't be made on an empty stomach."

The door opened. It was Joey carrying the water bucket. "Only one egg broke."

"Well, that's real good," said Ida. "Bring 'em on in here, honey."

Chapter 32

Max stewed in his fury. But for the first time he felt fear. His left arm was scraped raw where the hatch had dragged from his elbow to his wrist. The skin was an angry red and a few beads of blood dotted the skin. His arm throbbed to the beat of his heart.

Max paced the attic floor like a caged lion. His anger blurred any capacity for reason left in his brain. They had to die, every one of them. He could abide no other outcome. The problem was, he didn't really have a plan to achieve that goal. He'd planned to burn them all in their beds the night before, but Ida got the drop on him first.

"Fucking cunt." He shook his head.

He felt as if the vaulted ceiling were closing in on him. He stared at the hatch, then out through the window overlooking the porch roof. The dismal winter scene of swirling snow and the dark shadowed forest beyond did nothing to bolster his mood. The window was too small for him to climb through. Anyway, the window didn't open, and if he tried to break it, they would hear him downstairs.

Max's stomach rumbled. He could still smell the fried bacon and what smelled like scrambled eggs and toast. His mouth watered at the memory of the delicious bread Ida had baked yesterday. He was certain they weren't going to feed him now. He couldn't blame them. They weren't going to open the hatch on his promise not to attack them. He laughed hollowly. The sound startled him into silence.

Don't crack up now, Max.

Think. How could he get out? How long could they keep him locked up here? His eyes kept coming back to the window. It was about twelve inches square, maybe slightly bigger. Max scrunched up his shoulders, to gauge how narrow he could make himself. The movement sent searing pain up and down his injured arm.

"Motherfucker!" he spat and jumped to his feet. He kicked the bed over. The side rail he'd kicked broke loose. His engineering background brought his eyes back to the window. It was framed into the walls with short sections of log set vertically on either side of the window. This was to support the long logs above it, to keep them from settling down on the window as the wall logs dried and shrank. The side logs were each about six inches wide.

An idea crept in his mind.

Chapter 33

Gigi purred as she ate her eggs and crumbled bits of bacon. When she'd finished, she licked her lips, took a few delicate laps from her water bowl, and then sauntered over and leaped into Ida's lap.

Ida stared into the flames. The wind howled outside, rattling the windows, and tugging at the eaves. Swirling snow beat against the glass, collected on the sills, and then blew away again.

Ida's thoughts drifted to the precious stolen moments with Maggie. In those brief snippets of time, her single objective had been Maggie's happiness, to be its cause, to witness joy in her eyes. In Maggie's company, Ida had been complete. But then her reverie died, infiltrated by images of darker events that shattered the quiet moment, plunging her heart to new depths of sorrow and emptiness. Maggie was lost to Ida and time. There was no going back to her. Ida concentrated instead on the realization that she had, at last, likely come to the end of her long-endured imprisonment, a sentence she fully acknowledged she'd inflicted on herself.

Could it really be true?

So many times before, she'd thought she was nearing the end only to wake and find herself repeating the movements yet again. She cast her eyes around the cabin. It was like the set of a play—not that she had ever attended one. Her possessions, like props, were collected and meticulously set in their places, ready for the next performance. Though she supposed most of life was that way really.

She imagined her tiny farm viewed from above—a tranquil scene contained within its own little bubble, separate from the rest of the world. The constant hope exhausted her.

But it was nearly done—she was certain of it. But time was running out. They'd have to act soon. Ida stood up, gently setting Gigi down on the floor. She reached over and picked up the poker to stir the fire.

"Joey, could you come over here and sit with us, please?" She spoke quietly, shooting a glance at the ceiling.

"Sure," said Joey.

Ida finished fussing with the fire "You have to leave today. This mornin'. Time's almost gone."

Rhonda was shocked. She cast a sidelong glance to the window at the ground blizzard raging outside. "In that?"

Joey wanted to leave. He wanted to get to his aunt Elizabeth's house. He was excited by his mother's plan to leave his father, to live with his aunt. But at the same time, he didn't want to say goodbye to Ida. He felt safe with her.

"Is something going to happen?" Joey asked.

"Yes," said Ida. "And you can't be here when it does. If you are, you won't be able to leave again. At least, not for a very long time." She paused a moment. "If you left anything upstairs, you'll just have to leave it. We can't give Max a chance to get loose. If that happens, everything's lost."

In spite of the terrible weather, Rhonda knew that it was time to leave. But how could they make it to the car through all that snow? It was at least a mile, maybe more, and the car was stuck. And what would they do if they made it that far? Surely it was safer to wait out the storm here in this warm cabin, rather than freeze to death in the car. It seemed unlikely that someone would come along and rescue them.

"This makes no sense," Rhonda said. "What could possibly happen that would make returning to the car a better option than waiting here?" For a brief moment, Rhonda questioned Ida's sanity.

"You ain't where you think you are," replied Ida.

Rhonda said nothing.

"I can't explain to you just where we are because I don't know for certain myself. But it's important you understand that it's not a permanent place. It won't last much longer. It opens for a while, and then it just winks out again. If you're here, you'll wink out with it," explained Ida.

"What about you?" asked Joey.

Ida considered the question.

"I go with it," she said at last. "But I come back again. I don't know where I go—it's like I just go to sleep. Then I wake up again, and it all starts over when new visitors show up." She cast a glance at the ceiling. "'Course, this time might be different."

"How can this be?" Rhonda stared at Ida.

"Don't know," replied Ida. "But you've got to believe it is."

"What about Max? What happens to him?"

There was no sugarcoating her reply. Ida said, "He's lost."

"Do you mean that he'll die?" asked Joey.

Ida stared into the flames. "I don't know. All I know for sure is that he won't stay here, and he won't be coming back to your place. The Teeka will take him. But I don't know where."

"Why would it take him?" asked Rhonda.

"Why?" asked Ida. "Because he's worthy."

Chapter 34

Max lay sprawled on the floor. He held his injured arm to his side, wincing at the fresh pain it caused. Through a narrow crack in the floor, he heard the others talking in the room below. His stomach was a shriveled ball, and pangs of hunger stabbed through him. When their voices drew quiet, he became suspicious.

Fucking mumbo jumbo, he thought, though he couldn't deny they had the upper hand.

And what the fuck did she mean by *worthy*? Worthy of what?

When their little meeting adjourned, Max hefted himself to his feet and sat on Joey's bed. He tried to keep as quiet as possible. Best to keep them guessing what he was up to. Regardless, he knew they had no intention of letting him out of the attic. So, it was up to him to liberate himself. He thought he had a way. That side rail from the broken bed was thick and heavy. It would make an ideal battering ram against the side supports of the little window. That would widen the opening enough for him to escape.

Ida had said that Rhonda and Joey had to leave soon, or they'd be stuck here. But Max had the car keys. He patted his pants pocket, first the left side, then the right.

"Fuck." He remembered tucking the key fob into his coat pocket as they left the car to follow the light in the woods.

Well, it didn't matter. They would look for the keys before they left and find them. He was sure of it. And Max would take them back from Rhonda's cold, dead hand. The thought made him giddy. Freedom was so close now. He'd have his life back, all to himself. He could do anything he wanted, and he planned to. No more goddamn leeching family holding him back, sucking the joy from his existence.

Now he just needed to be patient. He would have to wait until they left the cabin before he could break out and track them down. His only concern at this point was the shotgun. Would Ida follow them out when his wife and son left? Would she take the gun with her? Would she watch them depart from the warmth and comfort of the cabin? He didn't know, but he was prepared to act quickly. From the urgency of the chatter below, Max guessed he didn't have long to wait. And he was right.

Chapter 35

Ida broke open the breech of the shotgun and reloaded it. Then she bent down and stroked Gigi. "Good-bye, sweet one," she said, and opened the door a crack and let her out.

Ida shuffled across the cabin, carrying the shotgun in the crook of her arm. "Take this," she said. "Get used to the heft of it."

Rhonda took the offered gun, though she'd never held one before. It was heavier than she thought.

"Aim it," said Ida, pointing toward the front door.

Rhonda never liked the idea of guns. She certainly never wanted to hold one. But as she stood there, raising the barrel and snuggling the butt against her shoulder, the way she'd seen Ida do earlier, she felt a sense of confidence like nothing she'd ever experienced before in her life. It was a dangerous feeling, because it gave her a sense of invulnerability that she knew was an illusion.

"You point it and squeeze the trigger," instructed Ida. "You don't need to aim too good. Just be sure it's pointed in the general direction." She didn't say, "pointed at Max," but the meaning was clear.

"What about you?"

Ida smiled, "I won't be needin' it anymore. And I still got my daddy's huntin' rifle stored under my bed." She patted Rhonda on the arm. "Now, you need to go. Time's 'bout up."

Ida waited patiently by the front door.

Rhonda handed the shotgun to Ida so she could pull on her coat before suddenly remembering she didn't have the car key. Max did.

"Oh, the key!" she exclaimed. Her face fell. Even if they managed to get back to the car, without the keys they weren't going anywhere.

"Check his coat pockets," Joey said. "He always leaves his key fob in his coat pocket."

"It's true," said Rhonda, searching through Max's coat. "Ah, here it is!" She pulled the key fob out, holding it like a trophy.

"That's good, honey," said Ida, distracted. She was anxious for this to end, for them to be on their way.

Joey was shrugging his coat on when a terrible crash came from the attic above them. It was wood wrenching against wood, followed by silence.

"What was that?" exclaimed Rhonda, her hand on the door as if to steady herself.

"I think he's gettin' restless," answered Ida. "Best to hurry now." She handed the gun back to Rhonda. Joey quickly pulled his coat on and zipped it up.

"Thank you so much," gushed Rhonda, hugging Ida.

"Honey, get to the car as quick as you can. You'll be safe once you get to your car."

Rhonda nodded and opened the door.

Wind rushed into the cabin as Rhonda stepped out onto the porch.

"Goodbye, honey," Ida said to Joey.

"I hope you'll be all right. It doesn't feel right leaving you here with him."

"Get back to the car. You'll be out of here when you reach the car. You'll be back on your side, where you belong."

Joey wiped tears from his eyes. "Goodbye."

"Goodbye, honey."

As Joey stepped out the door, Ida shut it behind him.

"Ready?" asked Rhonda.

Joey nodded.

The snow was deep.

"Oh my God," said Rhonda. She staggered forward, the butt of the gunstock slipping from her arm and dragging through the snow beside her.

Joey followed closely behind his mother. He could see how badly she was struggling. "Mom, I can go ahead of you. I think I can break the trail faster."

Rhonda agreed.

"Should I wait for you?" asked Joey, glancing over his shoulder.

"No! You go as fast as you can. I'll catch up."

They both stopped abruptly when they heard the sound of shattering glass.

Chapter 36

They're leaving. Max heard them talking downstairs, then the door opening and closing. They were escaping. He looked out the window and saw Rhonda emerging from under the porch roof carrying the gun.

"Fuck," he said, picking up the bedrail he'd wrenched loose from the bed frame a few minutes before. "Gun or no gun, you're not getting away."

Max stood back a few feet from the wall and heaved the bed rail at the window like a battering ram. The ancient glass, full of ripples and waves distorting the scene beyond, exploded outward. The rush of wind flooding through the opening chilled Max instantly. His mind flashed to his coat on the hook downstairs, and he swore again. It was going to be very cold without it.

Can't be helped, he thought.

At the sound of the breaking glass, Rhonda and Joey turned to look up at him. He grinned. Even from his perch in the attic, he could see the fear on their faces.

"That's right, bitch. I'm coming for you!" he yelled out the window.

Max was about to attack the side supports of the window to make the opening big enough for him to squeeze through when an unexpected thing happened.

Scrape.

It was the sound of the deadbolt on the hatch sliding back.

"What the fuck?" Why would Ida unlock the hatch? *Could be a trap*, he mused. But he was already trapped, so what sense did that make?

Max dropped the bed rail with a clatter and walked cautiously over to the hatch covering the stairs. He stared down at the knotted rope handle poking through the hole in the wood.

"Ida?" he called out. "Having a change of heart?"

No reply.

"Well, fuck."

Perhaps Ida had another gun, or was waiting to attack him with a knife. Max listened for noises downstairs, but nothing stirred—all he could hear was the wind blowing through the shattered window.

Max stared out the window to check on Rhonda and Joey's position. He saw they were making good progress. Joey was breaking trail at a furious pace. They had rounded the stacked pole fence, its sharp zigzag line dulled and softened by the deep snow drifted over it. Now they were making their way down the lane at the edge of the forest.

"Fuck it," said Max, making the decision to try the hatch. If he could go down that way, he'd be able to grab his coat on the way out. His wife and son's progress had lit a spark in him. He didn't want them to get too far ahead. What if someone had found the car? It seemed unlikely. After all, the road where they'd left it didn't go anywhere. There would be no reason for anyone to be there.

Unless someone was coming to check on Ida.

She'd said that no one came to her cabin, but she could have been lying.

Max tugged the rope handle and began to open the heavy oak hatch. He half-expected a shot to ring out.

Nothing happened. Max lifted the hatch and peered down the stairs, but there was no sign of Ida.

"I don't want to hurt you," Max called down the stairs. He was lying. He'd like nothing more than to wrap his hands around Ida's throat and throttle the life out of her. But he was in a hurry.

Max had to catch up with Rhonda and Joey before they got too far away. He could always come back after he finished with them and deal with Ida.

There was only silence below.

Max took a tentative step down, the wooden tread creaking against his weight. He took another and bent over as he descended so that he could scope out the cabin interior. Nothing stirred. He didn't see Ida anywhere.

Maybe she was in the outhouse or checking the animals in the barn. He knew she hadn't gone with his wife and son. He'd seen only the two of them making their way toward the woods.

As he stepped off the last stair and onto the cabin floor, he saw that the interior of the cabin was deserted.

Even the cat was gone.

The air still smelled of fried bacon, and Max's stomach lurched with hunger, but he ignored it. There was no time. Confident that Ida wasn't in the cabin, Max quickly crossed the room and grabbed his coat off the peg. Pulling it on, he checked the pockets for his car key, which was gone. Not a surprise. He figured Rhonda would have thought of that.

He lifted the latch and pulled the door open.

Stepping out onto the front porch, Max staggered back at the force of the frigid wind. Even with his heavy winter coat, the cold stabbed through him. "Damn, that's cold!" He hurried down the steps to the trail Rhonda and Joey had left for him, leaving the cabin door wide open behind him.

Max could barely make out his wife and son through the blizzard. They were now entering the trees where the trail began to wind its way through the forest. He felt that tickle of panic again. They were too far ahead. He wouldn't be able to catch up. But the trail was well broken from their passage, and he began a stumbling jog down the beaten path.

Max flinched at the loud bang behind him. He was sure he'd been shot. When he turned around, he saw that the front door of the cabin had slammed shut. Could a draft through the broken window have caused the door to close? Or had Ida done it? He found his answer when he looked to the left of the door and glimpsed Ida in the window. She was staring at him, a smile on her face. Max realized she must have been hiding somewhere in the cabin.

Ida's smile chilled Max's heart, but he couldn't stop to ponder it now. He had to catch up with Rhonda and Joey. He didn't think his wife would be able to muster the nerve to shoot him. She'd always been a skittish bitch, frightened of her own shadow. The thought of her taking a shot at him seemed far-fetched. Still, he couldn't afford to take any more chances at this point. He'd have to be careful when he got closer.

He'd look for a branch along the way, something he could use as a club or a projectile. He liked the idea of a club.

As he hurried along the path, Max didn't notice the sporadic stomping and grunting in the forest. And he'd completely forgotten about the dark, shifting mass of menace he'd seen when he went out for the firewood the night before, so focused was he on his impending revenge.

Chapter 37

Ida emerged from the tight little closet under the stairs where she'd hidden herself away after sliding back the deadbolt on the hatch to the attic. Max had probably wondered why she would do such a thing, never thinking that she'd wanted him to escape. But he wasn't vulnerable in the cabin. He had to be outside. And she had to offer him up to the Teeka. That was how this worked.

Ida wanted to give Rhonda and Joey more time to put some distance between themselves and the cabin. She knew Max would be cautious, reluctant to race down the stairs and out of the cabin. She'd been right, and it had given Rhonda and Joey a head start.

Ida stood in the open doorway and peered out. Max was following Joey and Rhonda's trail, his wife and son barely visible through the ground blizzard. Ida slammed the door shut to give Max pause for a moment, buying Rhonda and Joey another second or two. She stood by the window. She saw him turn and see her. She smiled, though it was still too early for celebration. She couldn't help it. She'd never been this close before.

Alone in the cabin, Ida felt the loneliness of the decades creeping back into her heart—she shooed them away like a pesky fly.

Won't be too much longer.

Ida wondered what it would feel like. Would it be like before, here one minute and winked out the next, only to wake again years or decades later? Or would it be something else? Merely a continuation of her day and her life? She had never gotten beyond this day before, so she truly had no idea what to expect.

Ida didn't think Rhonda would actually shoot Max. She didn't believe Rhonda was capable of such violence, not even in these circumstances. Which was good, because Max was useless dead, or at least dead before he was judged.

This was the most delicate phase.

Ida wouldn't miss the shotgun. It wasn't hers anyway. It was a relic left by the last couple who stumbled into her hollow. Neither of them had been worthy. She didn't know if they'd made it back out or went somewhere else. She only knew that shortly after they had gone, the darkness had come again, like the blackness of a moonless night quickly swallowing the world.

All Ida could do now was wait. Ida was good at that. And now she knew just how good at it she really was. She'd asked Rhonda the date when they first arrived on her doorstep. She had to admit she'd been shocked. She marveled that it had taken so long for someone to find their way to her cabin again. Eight years is a long time to sleep. Of course, she'd been waiting for well over a century in total. Ida couldn't even imagine what the world would look like now, outside her little hollow. She didn't think she'd like to know either. But she wouldn't mind some companionship. She looked at the long years ahead, if the debt was indeed paid, and how lonely they might be.

Chapter 38

After leaving the cabin, Joey noticed marks in the snow. At first, he wasn't sure what they were—he thought that perhaps they were left by his mother dragging the butt of the shotgun. Then suddenly he realized what they were. Cat paw prints.

It was Gigi. But he couldn't understand why she was out here or where she was going.

Rhonda and Joey heard the cabin door slamming shut. Even at this distance, with the wind filling the void between them, it startled Joey and his mother. They turned and saw Max chasing them along the trail Rhonda and Joey had made. He was charging at them, fast.

"GO! GO! GO!" shouted Rhonda. She scrambled after Joey as he ran, stumbling and weaving to break trail through the woods.

There was no sign of the trail they made the day before when the snow had only been a foot deep, although there seemed to be a natural path through the trees. Joey hoped they were going in the right direction. The cat paw prints seemed to be heading in the same direction they were. That gave him confidence.

The wind barreled like a freight train down the mountain. The force was staggering, nearly knocking them to the ground.

Rhonda didn't dare look back. The shotgun was weighing her down, but she couldn't abandon it—they had no other defense. She was determined to use it only as a last resort. Maybe they would make it to the car and get away before Max emerged from the forest. She knew it was unlikely. The car had been stuck in less than a foot of snow yesterday. She couldn't imagine the effort it would take to free it now with several feet of snow blocking it.

It felt like they'd been running for hours. They were both exhausted, sweat streaming down their faces despite the bitter cold wind. Clouds of panted breath fogged around their heads. Rhonda chanced a quick look over her shoulder. A jolt shot through her. She was horrified to see that Max was gaining. He was still a fair bit behind but had halved the distance between them. Digging down deep, Rhonda searched for any reserves of energy she could find.

Seeing into the forest ahead of them, Rhonda was confused. Something was wrong. The daylight was draining away from the woods as if night were falling even though it was still morning. She felt dizzy. Her leg muscles screamed at her to stop running. She couldn't do it. She had to get Joey out. They had to make it. She couldn't allow Max to win. Not this time.

The crashing and stomping sounds returned. It was the same as before, at the outhouse—heavy and threatening. Rhonda's heart hammered in her chest as she pounded out more speed. Joey was pulling away from her, and she ran with all her might to catch up.

The wind whistled through the treetops. Max had closed the distance and was only a few dozen yards behind them.

"Mom, the gun!" Joey shouted.

"I'm going to kill you, you fucking bitch!" Max shouted as he drew closer, his voice surging and waning in the wind. He'd run full-bore for nearly half a mile. And now he looked spent. He stopped and rested his hand on a tree for support, leaning over, and panting. But his eyes never left his wife and son.

"Stay away, Max," Rhonda shouted. "Please, Max, just let us go!"

The crashing and stomping in the forest ceased, as if pausing to see how this confrontation would play out. High above in the treetops, the bare branches twisted in the wind like rattling bones.

Rhonda turned to face Max straight on. She raised the shotgun to her shoulder the way Ida had shown her. Joey watched as his mother aimed the gun at his father.

"Please, Max. Don't do this. Just go back. I don't want to do this."

Max glared at his wife. He stood up straight and grinned a predator smile at her.

"You've always been a sniveling coward," spat Max. He took a few steps through the snow toward Rhonda. "You haven't got it in you."

Rhonda watched as Max took step after step, slowly closing the distance between them.

"Don't," she pleaded one last time.

Max took a few more steps. He knew Rhonda wouldn't pull the trigger. She had never pulled the trigger. He remembered the doctor prodding her for the truth when she'd lost the baby. She hadn't pulled the trigger then. She was a weak, pathetic coward, and he was looking forward to the excruciating pain he was about to inflict on her.

This is going to be so satisfying.

Rhonda aimed the shotgun at Max. He was only twenty-five feet away now. And as she pointed the gun at her husband, she found that she couldn't pull the trigger. No matter what he'd done, she didn't have it in her to take someone else's life, to be the one responsible for ending his existence.

She trembled, frustrated that she was failing to protect Joey once again.

Joey watched his mother. He knew she wouldn't shoot his father. It wasn't cowardice. It was who she was.

Rhonda lifted the shotgun above her head and threw it into a bank of snow.

Joey's heart sank as he watched his mother throw the shotgun away.

"I'm sorry, Joey. I couldn't do it."

Joey took her hand and pulled her along as he ran. "Come on!"

They had made it only a few yards farther before Max's deep voice echoed through the trees. "Stop!"

Joey and Rhonda lurched to a halt.

Max walked toward them, the shotgun hefted and aimed directly at his wife and son.

"You're such a fuck-up," said Max. "You can't do anything right."

"Please, Max! Just let us go," Rhonda pleaded.

Joey, silent and defiant, stared at his father.

Max gestured at Joey with the barrel of the shotgun. "Step away from your mother."

"No."

"Step away or she gets it in the head." Max stepped forward, the end of the barrel now only ten feet away from them and pointed at Rhonda.

Joey broke his mother's embrace and stepped away to her right.

"That's far enough," said Max when Joey had moved about six feet away.

Max turned the shotgun on Joey now. "I figure this will hurt you the most," he said to Rhonda, as he aimed the barrel of the gun at Joey's chest. "Besides, I have other plans for you. Slower plans."

"No!" she screamed and lurched to block Joey from the blast of the gun.

Max pulled the trigger.

Rhonda stood in front of Joey, her heart pounding. The gun hadn't fired.

Rhonda flashed back to the cabin, Ida loading the gun at the front door. She realized Ida had only been going through the motions for Rhonda's peace of mind. She had never loaded the gun at all! She knew Rhonda would never pull the trigger, but Max would if he got ahold of it.

Max was stunned. He pulled the trigger again and again, with the same dry click each time. Finally, he roared in frustration and raised the shotgun like a club.

Joey shouted, "Mom! Run!"

Max was ready to beat his wife and son to death with the shotgun.

A darkness descended, and with it a roar of shrieks, tornadic wind, and something else. The stomping returned. It was everywhere, on every side of them, impossibly above them—the sound like giant redwoods slamming to the earth from dizzying heights, or dark worlds collapsing into each other, colliding. It filled their minds, the amplified thundering reverberated through their bodies, their skulls, like a bass drum.

And the world seemed to disappear, the weak light of day instantly displaced by an inky blackness. The snow seemed the only source of illumination. Rhonda looked back. She could faintly make out Max's form a few steps behind her. He'd stopped advancing on her. He was spinning in circles, frantically, desperate to find the source of the cacophony. The useless shotgun was lost somewhere in the snow, forgotten.

The stomping ceased, and the horrifying swirl of air that Joey and Rhonda had each experienced in the outhouse descended on Max.

"What the fuck?" screamed Max. He was batting at the air as if engulfed in a swarm of hornets.

"Mom!" screamed Joey, clutching at his mother. She grabbed him into a hug as they watched Max battle his invisible foe.

Max slapped at tiny stings to his face. It was like every stinging, biting, scratching creature on the planet was attacking him. He felt spiders crawling under his skin, burrowing down, ever deeper, into the softer tissues and organs, and finally tunneling into his bones. Max's screams of agony and terror filled the dark forest. He began to dissolve. A swirling, roaring wind slammed through the trees and then suddenly stopped with a shriek.

And then there was silence.

Rhonda and Joey clung to each other. There was now only a faint glow in the woods. Max was gone and the several feet of snow was now only a couple of inches deep.

"Mom?" Joey asked. "What's happened?"

"Sweetheart, I don't know." Rhonda squinted as she saw a light up ahead. "Are those headlights?"

"I think so," replied Joey.

A few hundred yards away two bright discs of light shone through the forest. Rhonda and Joey walked toward them.

Part Three

Reunions

Chapter 39

Elizabeth sat in her idling Bronco. She'd parked at an angle behind her brother-in-law's car at the end of the dirt road, precisely where she'd intended it to be.

On the surface, the story brought to her attention seemed outlandish—at the most charitable, at worst, ridiculously impossible. But as a professor of Appalachian Folklore, she liked to believe she kept an open mind. When Miss Gortham, first an interviewee and then a good friend, told her the story, Elizabeth was ready to try anything to liberate her sister and nephew from Max.

She'd seen and heard about the bruises from his fists. And the psychological deterioration of both Rhonda and Joey from the constant reign of terror Max inflicted on them. And it had to stop before Max took it to the next level, which Elizabeth had been certain was quickly approaching. And then Rhonda had told her about the life insurance policies she'd found in Max's desk. She knew she was out of time. She had to act.

The snow had let up soon after Elizabeth and Miss Gortham drove into the Hollows, with only a couple of inches of accumulation. Her plan had been predicated on Max getting his car stuck. The promised snow didn't seem likely to be enough. Miss Gortham, however, was more than confident that wouldn't be a problem.

It will be provided, were Miss Gortham's words.

The relief was palpable when Elizabeth guided her Bronco around that last tight curve in the road and saw Max's car stuck in the light snow cover.

Elizabeth inspected the area around the car in the glow of her own headlights. She saw the trampled snow where Rhonda, Joey, and Max had tried to push the car out. She also saw the footprints leading into the woods and knew that at least the first part of her plan had succeeded. The second part relied entirely on the efficacy of Miss Gortham's story, which Elizabeth still couldn't fully believe or understand. But she had hope and faith in Miss Gortham.

She laid her hand on the hood of Max's car and felt the heat still radiating off it. They hadn't been gone long. Searching the forest, she could see nothing but light snow cover and naked trees, like wandering phantoms in the dark. Miss Gortham climbed out of the Bronco and joined Elizabeth.

She gently squeezed Elizabeth's arm. "Your sister and Joey will be fine."

"What do we do now?"

"You wait," replied Miss Gortham. She started walking into the woods, following the tracks in the snow.

"I don't understand why I can't come with you." This part of the plan left Elizabeth uneasy. Miss Gortham wasn't exactly frail, but she was in her seventies. Also, Elizabeth wanted to meet Ida Wheeling. She was captivated by the very idea of her. She had studied pioneering women from the Appalachians for years, but this was different. Ida was different. If she were being honest with herself, Elizabeth wished she had lived in Ida's time. She would gladly give up her house and job at the university for this other life if there had been a choice.

"Your concern for your sister and Joey is commendable, but you are not a part of the equation, at this point at any rate," replied Miss Gortham, pausing at the edge of the forest. "Go back to the car. It won't take long." And with that Miss Gortham marched into the trees and was quickly swallowed by the darkness.

"Miss Gortham!" called Elizabeth. The swiftness of the woman's disappearance unnerved her.

Elizabeth returned to her Bronco and climbed in. She turned up the heater and waited.

Is this crazy?

Elizabeth met Miss Gortham a few years earlier, when Elizabeth was researching her last book on the subject of Appalachian folklore. They quickly struck up a friendship, and Miss Gortham finally shared the more guarded secrets she knew of the region, and her connection to them. Then she showed Elizabeth the journal.

Elizabeth had read the material with an open mind. Doing her own research, she discovered the accounts of other missing people, who later turned up with no recollection of what had happened to them or where they had been, going back over one hundred years. Elizabeth began to believe something was going on out here in the Hollows.

They'd obviously arrived shortly after her sister and her family had abandoned their car, and yet there was no sign of them, save their footprints in the snow. They couldn't have gotten very far into the woods. Elizabeth should have been able to see a flashlight beam or something. But there was nothing. And now Miss Gortham had done the same thing. It unsettled her how quickly the old woman had vanished.

"Okay, Elizabeth," speaking calmly to herself. "Let's give it a little while and see."

Elizabeth felt drowsy in the blasting heat of the Bronco's vents, so she climbed out of the car to cool off. Scanning the dark forest, her eyes caught a flicker of movement.

"Hello?" she called out. "Miss Gortham?"

"Yes, dear," came Miss Gortham's reply. Threading herself between the scrubby saplings at the edge of the road, she appeared out of the forest and clung, exhausted, to Elizabeth's arm.

"Come on, let's get you into the Bronco. You're shivering."

"Thank you," said Miss Gortham, as Elizabeth helped her into the warm vehicle. "I always forget how tiring coming back can be."

"Did something go wrong? You've been gone barely fifteen minutes." Elizabeth had a sudden vision of a furious Max charging out of the trees on a rampage.

"You should go watch for them. They should be coming out very soon."

Elizabeth climbed out of the car and hurried to the edge of the woods, watching out for her sister and nephew. She didn't have long to wait.

Chapter 40

"Come on, mom! I see our car! We're almost there." called Joey, coaxing his mother along. She had fallen back as her son dashed toward the lights shining into the forest. He waited until Rhonda caught up with him.

"I was dizzy," said Rhonda.

Joey held onto his mother. "Can you make it a little farther? I think someone's there. I think someone's found us!"

Rhonda held onto Joey.

"Almost there, Mom!"

As they stumbled the last few yards to the edge of the woods, a familiar voice welcomed them.

"Oh, thank God, you're back!" Elizabeth rushed forward to help her sister. "Come on."

Rhonda saw an older woman sitting in the front seat of Elizabeth's Bronco. "Who is that?"

"That's a long story," replied Elizabeth. "That's Miss Gortham. I interviewed her several times for my last book." Then something occurred to her. "Where's Max?"

Rhonda stumbled over her words.

"He's gone," said Joey matter of factly.

Elizabeth helped Rhonda to the rear door behind Miss Gortham.

"How long have you been out here looking for us?" asked Rhonda.

Elizabeth ignored the question as she settled Rhonda and closed the door. Joey had already climbed in on the other side. Elizabeth scrambled into the driver's seat, pulling the door closed and warming her hands in front of the heater vent.

"Elizabeth?" said Rhonda.

Miss Gortham spoke first, her voice tired, but confident, "Dear, you've been here less than an hour."

Rhonda was incredulous. "That's ridiculous!" She glared at Elizabeth. "We got stuck out here yesterday afternoon, because of the faulty directions you gave us." She was confused, and tired, and she couldn't steady her mind. She kept wondering why it was dark in the middle of the morning.

"I came to find you when I realized the mistake I'd made with the directions. I tried calling your phone, but there isn't any reception out here," said Elizabeth. "I stopped in town to pick up Miss Gortham because she knows this area well, in case I got lost."

Rhonda shook her head. "No! That's impossible! We got stuck yesterday and saw a light through the trees. We walked to Ida's cabin, in there." She pointed to the forest, the stark, bare trees, sinister and dangerous in the headlights. "She took us in."

"She was really nice to us," offered Joey. "Why is it nighttime? It was morning when we left Ida's cabin."

Nobody responded.

"We can go ask Ida," said Joey.

"Yes!" said Rhonda. "Her cabin is only about a mile through the woods."

Elizabeth shared a quick glance with Miss Gortham.

"Rhonda, sweetheart." Elizabeth spoke calmly, but sternly.

"Don't do that!" screamed Rhonda. Elizabeth had always used that tone with her when she thought Rhonda was being unreasonable or childish. It had always driven her crazy, especially now that she was a grown woman. It infuriated her.

Elizabeth recoiled. "I'm sorry, I know I've talked down to you in the past. That is not what I'm doing now. We will explain everything." She glanced at Miss Gortham. "I know this is confusing, but you did arrive here an hour ago."

Rhonda raised her hands in frustration.

"I know! I know," said Elizabeth, "But I also believe you were at Ida's cabin overnight. I know that sounds impossible, but it will make sense later."

"Fine," said Rhonda. "I'm willing to take your word for it. For now."

Elizabeth sighed. "Thank you, because there's something more immediate that we need to agree on. We're going to have to call the sheriff and report Max missing."

"Okay," Rhonda said.

"You and Joey need to agree on what you're going to tell them. I will tell them about accidentally writing out the directions incorrectly. And when I realized my mistake, we came looking for you."

Rhonda nodded. "So what do we say happened to us?"

"The simplest truth," replied Elizabeth. "You followed my directions. You got stuck in the snow trying to turn around at a dead end."

"You planned this whole thing, didn't you?" Rhonda's accusation hung in the air until Miss Gortham finally spoke up.

"Something had to be done," she said.

Rhonda nodded. "I'm sorry you had to do this. I'm sorry I couldn't bring myself to do something about him before it got to this point." She wiped away tears.

Joey hugged his mother. "What happened to Ida? Is she still here?"

Elizabeth glanced at Miss Gortham.

"No," said Miss Gortham. "She never was here exactly. She's been stranded alone in that cabin somewhere between the past and oblivion ever since she called down the Teeka and took her own life." She was quiet for a moment. "You shared the dreams."

Joey nodded. He understood that Ida was somewhere else in time. "Is she still stuck?"

Miss Gortham smiled. "I don't think so. You see, there were two objectives. One was to remove Max, your father, from your lives—that's why we planned for you to go there. The second reason was to release Ida. She drank the tea before she could be burned alive for witchcraft in that cabin so many years ago, and the Teeka put her in that other place. It took a worthy life to release her again, meaning the life of someone who truly deserved to die. Max took her place, releasing Ida to live out her life."

Rhonda was confused. "Can we go home?" she asked, looking at Elizabeth. "I'm so tired."

"We can go back to my cottage," said Miss Gortham. "I have a room prepared for you. We still have to call the sheriff. Don't worry, though, this will soon be over."

Elizabeth shifted the Bronco into gear, and headed down the road.

"Wait!" Rhonda cried out.

Elizabeth slammed on the brakes. "What is it?"

Rhonda wasn't going to spend another day in the same clothes. "Can you get our suitcases from the trunk of Max's car, please?"

Chapter 41

Rhonda sat in Miss Gortham's cozy living room sipping chamomile tea, the deliciously sweet herbal aroma soothing her shattered nerves.

Sheriff Randal Clint sat opposite her. He scribbled in his notepad. After reviewing what he'd written, he glanced at Rhonda with piercing blue eyes.

Summer-sky blue, thought Rhonda.

"Is that all you remember?" asked Sheriff Clint.

"Yes," replied Rhonda.

Clint was a big man, tall with dark hair beginning to go gray. He was somewhere in his early to mid-forties. His bulk, likely once solid muscle—and much of it still was—had begun to soften and sag in places. His face was round and rugged, and he had a kind manner about him that put Rhonda at ease.

Rhonda had been filled with dread and guilty panic, but the sheriff had been gentle in his questioning. She'd tried to convince Elizabeth and Miss Gortham not to call the sheriff. She'd wanted to wait until morning until she'd had a chance to settle into the story that she and Joey would tell. But they both rejected that idea. Miss Gortham made the call to the sheriff's office.

Glancing at his notes, Clint said, "So you thought you saw a light through the trees and hiked toward it." He was looking at her statement. "And then you lost sight of the light and became disoriented, and your husband, Max, told you to go back and wait at the car while he continued on, looking for that light you'd seen."

Rhonda nodded. It was the same story Joey had told him before Elizabeth took him up to the room Miss Gortham had made ready for him. He was exhausted.

"Yes," she said. "He must have gotten lost. I turned on the car and the headlights so he could find his way out again. I even honked the horn for a while. But he didn't come back. After a few minutes, Joey and I went back into the woods to search for him. We called and called, but he didn't respond. It was so quiet. And whatever light we thought we'd seen was gone. I suppose it was a reflection off the snow, from the headlights, maybe? We couldn't find him. There were tracks in the snow, but they seemed scrambled, and we couldn't find where they led. Finally, we started back to the car, and that's when my sister Elizabeth, and Miss Gortham arrived." Now tears welled up and trickled down Rhonda's cheeks.

"Well, I sent two deputies out there, right after Miss Gortham called the station. They found your husband's car. It was smart of you to leave the keys in it in case your husband found his way back. One of the deputies will bring it back to town this evening. They followed the tracks in the snow. The tracks ended, but my deputies searched all the way back to the ruins of an old cabin, about a mile from the road."

Rhonda bit her lip. Could Max have gone back to the cabin? Could he have survived whatever it was that had descended on him? The Teeka? She had no idea. She didn't know what had happened to him, and her face clearly expressed that.

The sheriff seemed satisfied that she knew nothing about what happened to her husband. "So, you didn't hear anything. A large animal maybe? Anything like that?"

"No, nothing," she said, shaking her head slightly.

"Okay," said the sheriff.

"Did they find him? Or any sign of him?" Rhonda leaned forward on the edge of her seat.

Sheriff Clint closed his notepad and sighed. "No ma'am, nothing so far. We've called off the search for tonight. It's too dark and cold out there to be safe. One of my deputies will be parked for the night where your husband's car was found in case he finds his way back on his own."

Elizabeth patted Rhonda's back, "Oh, sweetheart, I'm sure they'll find him tomorrow. He's a strong man."

Miss Gortham shook her head. "This is such a terrible thing."

Sheriff Clint nodded. "Yes, ma'am. I'm sorry I don't have anything more definitive to tell you right now."

Rhonda nodded.

"We'll be back out there in the morning, searching. I'd like you to stay in the area until we can wrap this up."

"They'll be staying here, with me," said Miss Gortham.

Sheriff Clint nodded. "That's fine. As I said, your husband's car will be at the station sometime this evening. You can pick it up anytime tomorrow. We have your cell phone number. I'll be in touch."

Rhonda shook the sheriff's hand. Miss Gortham walked the sheriff to the door. He had to duck his head going through the doorway, the cottage seemingly built for elves and fairies, and perfectly suited to the diminutive Miss Gortham.

"Such a terrible thing," Rhonda heard Miss Gortham say again.

"Yes, ma'am," replied the sheriff, as the door closed behind them.

Elizabeth set her cup on the coffee table and hugged Rhonda. "How are you doing?"

"I'm okay," she said. "How's Joey? I want to go up and see him."

Elizabeth patted Rhonda's hand. "He's sleeping. He crawled into bed as soon as I took him up to his room."

Rhonda sank into a chair. "Is this real? Did this really happen?"

Sheriff Clint and Miss Gortham stood outside on the front porch.

"Could be a bear attack," said Sheriff Clint. "But there's no sign of a struggle."

"Yes," replied Miss Gortham absently. She tugged her calico sweater tight around herself. "Sheriff, give my best to my sister."

The sheriff laughed. He knew he wouldn't get his aunt to talk to him about what had happened. She hadn't before. But at least the previous episode, eight years ago—back when he was still a deputy—had ended well enough. A local couple, parents of a troubled student at Miss Gortham's school, had gotten lost in the Hollows on an overnight backpacking and hunting trip. They had planned to shoot a turkey for

Thanksgiving. They were lost overnight, but eventually found their way to the road where a friend, who'd gone out to join them for the day, had discovered them. They were cold, hungry, scared, and dehydrated, but otherwise okay. However, they couldn't remember a single thing about what happened to them after they left their car, including what had happened to their backpacks and shotgun. Those had never been found.

"Yes ma'am, I'll tell her," said Clint. He paused on the top step, a cold wind whipping in around them like a lost spirit searching for a home.

"Do you think this is the last time this will happen, Aunt Gigi?" He didn't look at her. Instead, he stared at the trees swaying in the breeze along the road.

"Have a good night, sheriff," replied Miss Gortham, as she shooed him down the steps.

The sheriff shook his head and returned to his car. He was born and raised in Shepherd County, and its mysteries never ceased to intrigue him. This was one mystery, though, that he'd be glad to let fade away.

Every kid who grew up here knew the legend of Ida Wheeling and the Teeka—the monster that eats daylight and souls, and the caricature of a withered old woman, a shape-shifting witch, with warts on her face, a hooknose, and long scaly fingers, looking for children to eat was an unkind representation, he was sure. Parents used it to frighten their children into compliance. He'd never done that with his own children, though. *Too close to home.*

Miss Gortham watched the sheriff leave, the patrol car's taillights disappearing around the bend in the road.

Chapter 42

Rhonda watched Elizabeth stir the coals in the brick fireplace, adding fresh logs. After seeing the sheriff off, Miss Gortham shuffled across the living room and through an archway into a small nook of a study. The room was lined with shelves stacked with books. There was a Turkish rug on the floor. Tucked cozily into one corner was a well-worn easy chair with a small table beside it. An old-fashioned floor lamp stood behind the chair with a beaded lampshade.

Miss Gortham carefully retrieved a leather-bound volume from a high shelf and carried it out to the living room, held lovingly against her chest.

"You know the end of the story," she said to Rhonda.

Rhonda gazed up at the older woman with curiosity.

Miss Gortham gently handed the book to Rhonda, and said, "Now I think you should read the beginning."

Rhonda took the book, noting the aged leather was cracked and stained. There was nothing written or embossed on the cover or spine, just the wear of age and use.

"If you like, you may take it in the study to read," said Miss Gortham. "I think you'll find it quite comfortable in there."

Rhonda nodded. She glanced over at Elizabeth standing by the fireplace, her hands clasped across her chest. There was a sparkle in her eyes as she smiled at Rhonda.

"All right," said Rhonda.

"That's good, dear. I think you'll understand so much better once you finish reading that." Miss Gortham smiled at Rhonda and nodded toward the study. "I'll fix you a fresh cup of tea and bring it in to you."

"Thank you," said Rhonda. She walked into the study.

Rhonda set the book down on the table and settled herself into the easy chair. *Oh my God*, she thought. *I could sleep in this chair!* She switched on the lamp. A warm glow of light enveloped her. She opened the book. Miss Gortham and Elizabeth disappeared into the kitchen.

Rhonda began reading.

Maggie Gortham-Donovan –

October 5th, 1888 –

Father caught Ida and me yesterday. We were hidden in the barn, but not well enough. We were only kissing, but it was enough to enrage him, and he sent Ida away. He threatened her a devil's death if she ever came around again! I cried but could not protest; his anger and disgust took my breath away. I was more frightened than I have ever experienced before, but not for myself—for my dearest Ida. A devil's death, or what my grandmother called the witch's death, means burning alive until dead. In the cities this thinking has long ago passed, but we are most decidedly not in the city. We are deep in the isolation of the Appalachian Mountains. I fear we are not only cut off physically, but intellectually as well. The idea froze my heart in terror for her.

I am not to see Ida ever again, though I don't believe my heart can stand such a punishment. We are meant to be together. She is everything that completes me. But father has promised me to wed. I think it is vindictiveness, to bury my heart in sorrow until I break. He is the schoolteacher here in the Hollows, and I know he struggles for money, and it would be a relief to his burden if I were in another's house.

October 25th, 1888-

The man is hideous! I cannot do it! Father has matched me to Mr. Gordon Donovan, a farmer with little to show for his efforts, and a widower. He has buried his first wife only a year ago, and now I am to marry him and take his child, a sickly daughter named, Hanna—that I do not hate, but do not know—as my own. He leers at me in church, and I cannot bear the thought of what he will do when the bond of marriage has made me his property.

November 10th, 1888-

It is done. I am married. My heart is broken, and I fear I am already with child. Mr. Gordon, as he insists I call him, is insatiable. I am raw and cannot stand the sight of him.

February 4th, 1889-

I am beginning to present now. It has lessened Mr. Gordon's appetite. Thank the Lord!

I glimpsed Ida two days ago at the trading post. My heart stood still when her eyes met mine, but she is still terrified of my father, and she quickly finished her business and departed. The clerk made the horrid out-of-hand comment that Ida was a witch. This was a dangerous thing to hear him say, as he is likely not the only one who thinks it.

I wanted to explain that she simply used the natural ingredients that God has blessed our region with to heal people. But I knew this would only cast a shadow on myself as well, and so kept my silence. I felt myself such a coward.

February 30th, 1889-

Word came that Ida's parents died of a fever. Her father died first, three weeks ago, and then her mother two nights ago. Ida is alone now. Her mother and grandmother before her were both healers, though her mother didn't take well to the craft; she didn't have the skills for it. Her grandmother taught Ida everything she knows, but unlike her mother and grandmother, Ida does not enjoy the respect of her trade. I fear, now that she is alone in her cabin in Long Hollow, she will garner more suspicion. She has never accepted courting, and a woman alone is still thought to be an evil enterprise. I know her reasons, and I would follow her if I had a fraction of her courage, but I cannot.

March 3rd, 1889-

I worry for my child. I have had pain I don't believe is normal. There are no doctors nearby. The closest is in Monroy, a hard day's travel away. I have asked Mr. Gordon to allow Ida to visit, to attend to me, as she is a midwife. But he says no. I am certain that father never shared what he witnessed between us in his barn, but Ida's reputation has not improved regardless.

March 29th, 1889-

A heavy snow has come. It is nearly three feet deep outside our door. I fear we will lose some of the animals. I am claustrophobic in this narrow hollow.

April 7th, 1889-

It seems winter will never end! More snow today. We have dug deep canyons to reach and care for the animals. Mr. Gordon butchered a cow yesterday, as there is barely enough hay to last until spring.

April 10th, 1889-

Hanna died yesterday morning. This is such a sad day. She has been sickly since I've known her, but she was a delightful child. I shall miss her company. Mr. Gordon seemed not as upset as I would have guessed. Perhaps he had known she would not last and had steeled himself against the inevitability. She did not feel well the night before and she went to bed early. She was dead when Mr. Gordon went to check on her in the morning.

The burial is tomorrow. Snow has been cleared from her burial site, and a roaring fire built on the ground, to thaw it enough to dig the grave.

April 20th, 1889-

The pain has returned and is more intense than before. I have renewed my request that Mr. Gordon call Ida to visit. He seems less adamant against my request. I am worried about the child, but I also want so desperately to see Ida again.

Mr. Gordon no longer tries to have intercourse, but he makes me do other things to raise him to his joy—as he calls it. He disgusts me. He is wicked and dirty in his mind and his body.

May 5th, 1889-

SPRING! So lovely today! The snow has all but melted, and green is returning to the mountains. The flowers are glorious! And Mr. Gordon has agreed to call on Ida to come to our house! I am so happy today!

May 14th, 1889-

There was blood today in my undergarments. But the baby is still moving. I am afraid. Mr. Gordon did not call on Ida as he said he would. But he is doing so now. He has gone there, and I pray she comes soon.

May 15th, 1889-

The isolation has been hard on Ida. She came last evening, following behind Mr. Gordon on her own horse. She has aged since I saw her last. Her hair is fading from the lovely blonde to silvery-gray now, and her soft, beautiful face appears so harsh. But when she saw me, her smile brightened the room more than the sun ever could!

Mr. Gordon wanted to stay. He is a perverted man. Ida insisted that she'd not have him there to distract her from her examination. He relented.

She says the baby is fine, which settles my mind immensely. Her hands on my body, as she checked my health, lit a fire I'd forgotten could exist! No matter how hard the winter has been on her, she is the most beautiful creature on earth!

She made arrangements with Mr. Gordon to come again in a week to make sure I was fine. He agreed, I think in no small part, because Ida held her tongue when he grabbed her bottom as she was leaving my room. I was shocked, as he did it in my sight. He thinks he might take her, but he doesn't realize when he is being played a fool. The very definition insists a fool does not know he is one.

May 22, 1889-

Ida came again today. She was frightened, and I must admit that I am frightened for her as well. There have been a rash of cattle deaths in the Hollows and the ignorant people here are eyeing her to lay blame. There is a school here and yet the people are ignorant and incurious. They cling to superstition and wives' tales, I suspect more to excuse their own laziness of mind than true conviction.

Ida confided that she had considered leaving the region. But ultimately could not bring herself to do so, saying, this is my home. She confided that she has had two visits in the night to her farm in the last week. There was an unsuccessful attempt to burn her barn, and many of her chickens were slaughtered. She fears for her life now. I am desperate to help her, but what can I do? I am pregnant and have no means of my own to offer assistance.

Despite her fear, and my own anxiety, she examined me more thoroughly than before, and it was heavenly. I'd never felt that level of ecstasy!

Before leaving, Ida confided that she had never harmed anyone or any creature in the way the rumors were suggesting, save butchering her own chickens, and a deer now and again, the same as everyone living in these wild mountains. But she has carried on her grandmother's pursuits in the more advanced art of unweaving nature's secrets. Her grandmother left her notes when she died, but Ida's mother never shared them. Ida has found them and has studied them extensively.

I must admit that some of what she told me seemed fantastical, and she frightened me with her enthusiasm. She claimed there were truths to the lore of the Teeka, though she did not claim to have seen it. But she did believe there were places alongside our own natural world, pockets, she called them, where one could live in the same place but separate from the regular world. I did not fully understand all that she told me. But I must admit that the idea of living with her in such a quiet, ideal place, apart from the ignorance of those we live alongside now, is an inviting prospect.

She told me that she had drawn on her grandmother's recipes, as her grandmother always called them—for to call them spells was truly courting disaster—and she was certain she had found the proper balance of ingredients that would allow her to pass to this other place. I balked when she told me that in order to perform the transformation one had to die in this world as part of the recipe. Surely she was conjuring the devil to do this! Not at all she had said. It was simply using the natural forces to explore further than our mere eyes and ears would allow us. Though the invocation of the Teeka, to facilitate the journey, certainly lends credence to the notion of raising the Devil. However, I did not point this out, as her spirits were so high.

Mr. Gordon interrupted us then, saying we had visited long enough. He asked after my condition and Ida told him I would deliver a healthy child. He was relieved to hear it, but he also told Ida not to visit again. There was too much talk in the Hollows about her. He didn't want the stain to spread to his house.

June 30th, 1889-

The heat is unbearable! I am confined to my bed as I've had a recurrence of the pain from earlier in my pregnancy. Fortunately, Mr. Gordon moved me down from our loft bedroom in the attic space to the small storage room off the kitchen because he could not be bothered with all the climbing of stairs to tend to me during the day. My father sent my old bed from his home. It is a small, cramped space, but there is a window that I can open, and I am grateful to no longer be subjected to Mr. Gordon's snoring and smelly feet!

July 8th, 1889-

Something is wrong! The pain has doubled. There is spotty blood again. The birth should not be for another month, but I do not feel the baby will wait until then. The baby seems to have shifted. I begged Mr. Gordon to bring Ida again, but he is dubious.

August 7th, 1889-

My baby, Alice, was born three weeks early. We should both have died, but Mr. Gordon finally relented as my condition was beyond his simple abilities. He called on Ida, and she came. She brought her bag with its assortment of herbs and distillates. My memory is foggy from that day. I was hot with fever, and my mind suffered. I remember the pain and panic. But I also remember the soothing voice of my true beloved as she worked to ease my pain and comfort my mind. There was so much blood, the sight of it sending my panic soaring again. Then I remember nothing until I woke sometime later, though it could not have been too long, as Ida was still at my side.

This next is Mr. Gordon's account, though I am sure he embellished to skew the story to his own betterment in others' eyes.

Mr. Gordon says there was too much blood lost and that I died as the baby was pushed out of my body. He said there were no cries from Alice, that she was blue and still. Then Ida set drops from one of her bottles into Alice's mouth and blew life back into her. Her coughs and shrieks sent Mr. Gordon fleeing from the room, sure that Alice was possessed by the devil. He says when he returned with Pastor Everett, I was revived as well. He says the room was filled with the cloying, thick scent of sulfur. I do not remember smelling this, though I was not in a proper state to have thoroughly taken note.

Mr. Gordon and the pastor stayed away from Alice and me. I could see the fear in their faces as they watched Ida finish tending to my still bleeding regions. Even as I held Alice to my breast, I could see the fear in the men's eyes change to something more sinister. As Ida finished and packed her bag, she was quickly ushered out of the house and sent on her way.

Rumors grew and spread quickly within a few days of Alice's birth, and I fear now for Ida's life if she is not careful.

November 25th, 1889-

I have recovered well from Alice's birth. I was a month gaining my strength back, and Alice too. Though now she is strong and is a handful to manage. Mr. Gordon seems to dote on her, but he has never looked at me the same since Ida saved my daughter and me. But I have not heard much talk of Ida generally among our neighbors, and I am relieved for that.

December 14th, 1889-

I cannot fathom what has happened. My heart is crushed. I cannot write more as my tears are uncontrollable.

December 22nd, 1889-

Poor, sweet little Clara Grover was found dead, murdered! If not for our dry winter thus far, she might not have been discovered for months. But there has been precious little snow this winter, only an unrelenting cold.

I believed that talk of Ida had dissipated. I was wrong to surmise that it had been forgotten. She was at once convicted in the minds of our neighbors of this horrible crime, begging favors from the devil himself to bring my child and me back from the dead and now paying her debt by giving Clara's life in exchange. The ugliness of ignorance was on full display in our rural hollow, as Ida's own sister, Eugenia, accused her of witchcraft.

I do not know—Mr. Gordon would not say—who went after Ida. But an assembly of men converged at her cabin the following morning and set it afire with her cornered inside. Mr. Gordon told of—and this proves in my own mind that he was present, because his eyes told me he had seen this himself—the cabin burning and no shrieks of pain or fear issuing from within. But a great whirlwind of air erupted from above, like an invisible tornado, and descended on the cabin, whipping the flames higher and higher, causing the flames to launch to the sky. And the sky turned black, as day turned to night in an instant. And he says others then reported seeing Ida rising up through the flames and disappearing from sight. The event has caused a great dread of the Teeka, and several of our last few neighbors are packing to leave the Hollows.

December 27th, 1889-

I left Alice in the care of my father today. He was happy to spend time with his granddaughter. The weather has turned mild, but some of our neighbors insist that a big storm will descend on us soon. Mr. Gordon was busy in the barn with the hay when I approached him. I insisted that I required some time to ride, and breathe the mountain air after being shut indoors for weeks. He mumbled something to the effect of foolish woman but I did not take offense because he did not forbid me to go.

I guided one of our horses along the trails above our hollow and took the seldom-used trail that crosses over to Long Hollow, where Ida's cabin once stood. I could not stand to gaze upon the ruins of her home, knowing that she had spent her last terrifying moments there.

There was a place we used to meet, and I started in that direction. The last of the trail was too steep for my horse and I loosely tied her reins to a low branch, with thick, dry grass underneath. I had not been here since I became pregnant, and I realized it has been more than a year.

It is a protected spot, with exposed granite for a back near the top of the ridge. A birch grove grows there. The memory of their leaves ablaze in iridescent yellow—as though the bright sun of the day sprung directly from them—was a distant fancy from my last visit here. Water seeps out from just below the ridge in a lovely spring. There was a dry spot with tufts of grass and a sheltered nook in the rock where we would leave notes to each other.

I sat in the dead grass, my legs weary from the exercise, as I had not had so much exertion since the birth of Alice. The sun was warm on my face, and the chilly breeze was cut to nothing by the rocky ridge to my back and the trees at my sides. The view of the hollow was lovely but pierced my heart with sadness, knowing that Ida would never again see it with me, and that I would never see her again.

I turned absently and noticed the small wooden cigar box we left in the nook. I could not remember the last note left there, if it was hers or mine. I reached in and withdrew the box and held it in my hands a moment before drawing up enough courage to open it. And when I did, my heart nearly stopped. There was a note inside, and I recognized Ida's writing instantly.

I have pressed the letter here rather than copying it. It warms my heart to see her words, written in her own hand.

Rhonda turned the delicate page and a folded note slipped out onto her lap.

"Here's your tea, dear," said Miss Gortham, as she entered the room.

Rhonda startled slightly. "Thank you," she said. She looked at Miss Gortham with newly opened eyes.

"Yes, dear?" Miss Gortham asked, patiently.

Rhonda laughed nervously. "It really happened, didn't it? It's all real."

"Yes, dear," replied Miss Gortham, smiling sweetly. "Quite real. When you're done reading, come out by the fire and we can talk." She turned and walked silently out of the room.

Chapter 43

Rhonda peered out the window as fresh snow blew against the glass. She thought back to Ida's cabin as she glanced at the note that had slipped from the journal's pages.

Carefully unfolding the brittle, yellowed paper, Rhonda read Ida's words, picturing the woman's face as she did so.

My Maggie,

My time is short. I love you.

They are coming for me. I knew this was coming. I know I don't have to convince you, but I must say this for my own piece of mind that it has been put out in the world. I did not harm that poor child!

I packed things you will need in a small crate and moved them to the little springhouse next to the creek behind the barn. I don't think they will look for anything there, as it is sheltered from view in the trees.

I will make the tea, and I will drink it if there's nothing else to be done. I know you doubt it, but I know my grandmother's recipe will work. I will miss you like my own heart has been plucked from my chest, but I'm not going to let them win against me.

You raise that baby girl right! Don't let Mr. Gordon teach her to hate.

You can save me, at least from the darkness, but you'll have to find someone to take my place in death. And to do that, they'll have to be truly worthy of it, or it won't take. I left my recipes in the crate, along with whatever else I could think of that you might need.

I have to go now. It's a hike up to our spot, and I can't chance you not knowing how much I love you. I wish this were a different world. I wish we could have been together. Don't ever forget that! Don't ever forget me.

I love you,
Ida

Tears welled up in Rhonda's eyes as she refolded the letter and tucked it away in the journal. She turned to the next page. Confused, she flipped back to the previous page to check the date of the last entry there: *December 27th, 1889.* Then she flipped forward again, satisfied that she hadn't missed anything. The next entry was over three years later.

May 5th, 1892-

It's been a long while since I last felt the courage to write. Mr. Gordon died three years ago of a heart attack in the field. The farm was lost, not that it was worth much. Like most of the other places in the Hollows, the ground demands too much toil and yields so little in return. He had no savings, and his debts were high.

My father moved to Monroy a month before Mr. Gordon died. He took the job as principal at the new school there. They gave him a small cottage that has become a real home. The school in the Hollows had dwindled in students as farmers left the mountains for better opportunities elsewhere. I have moved to Monroy at my father's insistence. I have to thank him for looking out for us that much. I work at the school, too, doing whatever needs doing for its smooth operation. We share the cottage. It is tight, but we manage. I enjoy the atmosphere here. Father made sure that I was educated as a child, and I am heartened that he is adamant now that Alice shall have an education as well. We use the little study off the living room as her classroom.

June 2ⁿᵈ, 1892-

I was not prepared for the overwhelming sorrow that clutched my heart when I last wrote and again thought of Ida. In truth, I have had to keep her memory out of my mind since we left the Hollows, in an attempt to keep from falling into absolute despair. I miss her with all of my soul, and if it weren't for the daily joy of Alice, I should have no happiness at all.

Evidence, in the form of bloody rags and a torn piece of Clara Glover's dress, was discovered in the cabin of Ida's sister, Eugenia, and her husband Evan, a week or so after the attack on Ida. No one would breathe the words that they had let their superstitious minds cloud their judgment and that Ida was innocent of the crime of which they accused her. But it matters little now. There is no one left in the Hollows anymore, and I think that is the way it should be. Eugenia and Evan disappeared the day after Clara's body was discovered, gone in the night with their horse and wagon and whatever they could carry. No one has heard from them since.

I managed to visit Ida's farm shortly after I found her note at our spot on the ridge. I went alone while Mr. Gordon was cutting wood in the forest, though I suspect he was doing more drinking than cutting. He had taken a liking to liquor. Alice was down for a nap. I feared the whole way there, spurring my horse on faster than was prudent for the bad trail, that Alice would wake before I returned. But she did not.

I gathered the contents of the springhouse that Ida had left for me, keeping my eyes averted from the burned shell of her cabin, though the smell of charred wood still filled that hollow. I would not have been able to bear the sight of it, knowing my love had died there so terribly. I carried the items Ida left in a thick canvas bag, as the crate was too bulky to manage.

I have not yet read the material she left for me. The unlikely hope that it could lead me to her again is too improbable to sustain belief in that fanciful idea. When I returned home, Mr. Gordon had not yet returned, and Alice was only then beginning to stir. I quickly hid the bag of Ida's things in the back of my wardrobe, which is now at my father's cottage with me.

June 17ᵗʰ, 1892-

The bag in the wardrobe is like a magnet, drawing my attention every day, no matter where I am. After supper each evening, father retires to his study and leaves me to attend to Alice. I have resolved to put my sadness aside and see what she has left me.

June 18ᵗʰ, 1892-

I was overwhelmed when I first opened the bag. I had not paid much mind to what I placed in it while at Ida's. I was too focused on getting home before I was caught out. Now I marvel at how organized she left the items for me. Her "recipes" are extensive; there must be nearly a hundred of them, but there are a set of them tied together, separate from the others, that she left on top with a scribbled note: Maggie, this will set me free. Please don't leave me in the darkness.

My heart was heavy. But I persisted, and as I read through her instructions, I began to have hope. The "process" is relatively simple, given that the worst part has already occurred: Ida has taken her tea and died at the cabin, though her body was never found.

As I read, I began to realize that I would not get to see her again. The recipe is only to replace her soul in death with another who is worthy, to free her to live her life to its end. But it will be lived wherever she is now, not here, because here, she has already died.

It seems fantastical, certainly against the teachings of the Bible. But I have never felt any allegiance to the fables held within those pages. If there is a way I might bring her soul to rest, then I must do so, even if it is folly and only serves to act out the last wishes she asks of me. She brought my baby and myself back to life! I owe her this at the very least.

Among the items Ida left to me include the herbs and reductions called for in the recipes. I know them well for Ida and

I spent many hours together in the forest, and she made sure I knew every plant that we passed by, and its uses.

August 4ᵗʰ, 1892-

Alice came down with an illness. She had a fever and was lethargic. The doctor from town seemed perplexed and unconfident when he prescribed aspirin powder, strong tea and rest. It seemed insufficient and, alas, it proved ineffective. On the fourth day, I decided to try one of Ida's recipes that I found among the many she left me. The ingredients were among those she had provided, and so there was no need to forage for any of them.

It has worked! Only a few hours after I administered the tea to Alice, her fever broke, and by the end of the day, she was able to walk on her own!

September 23ʳᵈ, 1892-

I have had the recipe prepared for a month, save the addition of the most toxic ingredient. But the main ingredient, a person worthy of administering it to, has eluded me, until yesterday. A boy came to my office, as I now also have the job of nurse for the school. He displayed signs of violation and was very embarrassed to admit that the man hired to clean had been taking *him in the custodial closet in the basement. My fury was difficult to control. But my mind seized on this as the opportunity presenting itself at last! I only had to work out how I would get him and myself out to Ida's ruined cabin—as the worthy must be present there for the passageway to open. And it is there that the "herbs that never meet, from ridge and hollow" must be burned together to call the Teeka forward to facilitate the transfer.*

September 25ᵗʰ, 1892-

It was not to be. I had conspired to use the school's wagon to carry us to the cabin ruins, but another boy had come forward to my father and told him what the custodian had been trying to do to him. My father summoned the sheriff, and the man was arrested and taken away.

I should be relieved that such a monster is no longer among us, but my heart is devastated instead. When shall another be discovered, for surely he was the perfect candidate?

December 23rd, 1892-

I have found no other. I fear now that it will take years to fulfill my dedication to Ida.

June 7th, 1900-

Years indeed! I will never forget my beloved Ida, nor cease in my efforts to bring her peace, but I have focused on Alice now. She is growing, and it occurred to me that I might never have the opportunity to see my quest finished. I have begun to share stories with Alice, and I have begun to teach her the arts of healing that Ida herself taught me, for Ida saved Alice's life as well, and the task may very well fall to her in the end.

There were several blank pages in the journal after that. Rhonda flipped ahead to find the next entry was twenty years later and written by someone else—it was signed *Alice.*

There were only a few short entries in Alice's hand, but she seemed as dedicated to freeing Ida as her mother was. Alice documented five occasions when she thought she had found someone worthy of the Teeka's attention, but to no avail—four of them had made it to Ida's cabin, but were later found wandering in the forest, unable to recall why they were there.

After only a few pages, the handwriting changed again—this time the author was Georgina Gortham, daughter of Alice, and granddaughter of Maggie.

Like her mother before her, Georgina wrote few entries. Then Rhonda read the entry about Georgina meeting Elizabeth, her sister, while she was researching her book.

Miss Gortham had been contacted by Elizabeth about an interview relating to folklore. That's how they met. That was the last entry.

Rhonda knew what happened next.

Chapter 44

A knock at the door startled Rhonda. She hadn't noticed Elizabeth standing there.

"Oh, sorry," said Rhonda. "I guess I was tuned out for a minute."

"Cup of tea?" Elizabeth said.

Rhonda glanced at the cup Miss Gortham had given her. It was full, untouched, and cold.

"Yes, please. That sounds wonderful." She'd had enough of her own thoughts for the moment. She needed company.

Rhonda closed the journal and carefully set it on the table. She picked up the cup of cold tea and followed her sister out to the living room.

"Where's Miss Gortham?" she asked. The living room was empty.

"In the kitchen," replied Elizabeth. "We didn't want to disturb you while you were reading."

"Any word from Joey?" asked Rhonda glancing up the stairs.

"No." said Elizabeth. "Not since I tucked him in. He's in the small room at the front if you want to check on him."

"I'd like to," said Rhonda. "Be right back."

"I'll put the kettle on."

Rhonda climbed the stairs, noting that Max would hate this house. He wanted everything new, never used. She put him out of her mind, realizing she never had to consider what he thought or wanted again.

At the top of the stairs, she walked down a narrow hallway to the door at the end. Rhonda knocked on the door.

"Joey?"

"Yes?" came Joey's sleepy voice. "Come in."

Rhonda breathed a sigh of relief. *Max is gone,* she told herself. *Stop thinking about him.*

Joey's room was dark, but the porch light below cast a shadowy blue-gray glow into the room. The snow was falling, but Joey was tucked up in an old-style four-poster bed, the covers drawn up tight under his chin.

"Just wanted to say, good night," said Rhonda, fussing with the covers.

"Thanks."

"Is the porch light bothering you? I can turn it off when I go downstairs."

"No," said Joey, "I like watching the snow."

"Okay." Rhonda fidgeted with her hands. "Joey?"

"Yes."

"If you want to talk about your dad, I'm here."

"No, I'm good."

"Okay," she said. "I love you." Rhonda kissed Joey's forehead.

"I love you too, Mom."

In the spacious country kitchen, Elizabeth and Miss Gortham sat at a long wooden harvest table drinking hot tea. A third steaming mug sat on the table next to Elizabeth.

Rhonda joined them in a squeaky ladder-back chair.

Miss Gortham sipped from her cup. "Children are generally far more resilient than adults give them credit for."

Rhonda couldn't argue. She gingerly picked up her hot mug and took a sip. She cast her eyes around the kitchen. It looked like a movie set from the 1800's, which made perfect sense. That would have been when it was built. It seemed nothing had changed since the 1970's, when the refrigerator and gas stove had been added.

The wall between the kitchen and living room was lined, floor to ceiling, with wooden shelves crammed with pots, pans, dishes, and canned goods. There was an old hutch with two doors above, and three drawers below a counter of enameled metal. The counter was neatly lined with spices and canisters, and the glass panes of the two upper doors showed more of the same.

A heavy white enameled sink with an attached drainboard was mounted on the wall at one end of the room. The steel arched faucet hung directly on the wall above the sink. There was a dark spot in the sink under the faucet where decades of dripping hard water had worn away the enamel surface.

Taking a sip of her tea, Rhonda's eyes widened.

"Is it all right?" asked Miss Gortham. "I have other flavors if you'd prefer."

Rhonda smiled, reminiscing. "No, it's wonderful. It's what Ida served us. I'd never tasted Chamomile so fresh before in my life."

Elizabeth asked, "What are you going to do now?"

Rhonda thought for a moment. "I'm going to sell the Maryland house as soon as I'm legally able to. I hate that house, and without Max's job to worry about, there's no reason to stay there. I guess I'm hoping the invitation to come live with you is still open, now that the initial reason is gone."

Rhonda couldn't bring herself to say Max's name. *The sooner you forget him, the better,* she thought.

Rhonda continued. "I was never allowed to ask about the bank account, so I really don't know if we're in dire straits or sitting on easy street. I know it was unforgivable the way I allowed him to dominate me the way I did. I'm afraid there's something terribly broken in me. That's all I can think of. It's the only excuse I have."

Elizabeth hugged her sister.

"It's over now. You are not that person anymore. I see that. I think Joey has too. And of course, you and Joey are welcome to come live at my house. It's always been *our* house anyway."

"Thank you." Rhonda rested her head on her sister's shoulder. "Thank you for everything."

"You're welcome, my brave rabbit."

Miss Gortham glanced at the clock on the stove. "Time for bed, I think."

Rhonda nodded. "Yes, I'm exhausted."

"That's to be expected," offered Miss Gortham. "You've been through a tremendous ordeal."

Rhonda nodded. She suddenly felt the drain of energy of the previous night and glanced at her empty mug on the table.

Don't be ridiculous, she scolded herself. *You're just tired, and it's the same kind of tea, that's all.*

"Elizabeth put your things in the room next to the bathroom upstairs. The one closest to Joey's room," said Miss Gortham.

"Thank you," said Rhonda, heading for the stairs.

"Goodnight, Rhonda. I love you," said Elizabeth.

But Rhonda was already gone.

Chapter 45

Joey was startled awake by a noise downstairs. He thought it might be his mother coming up to bed, but then he heard it again. It was a thud in the entryway by the front door directly below his room. There was a moment of panic. He imagined his father somehow coming back to finish what he'd planned. But that fear evaporated when he heard the faint squeak of the front door hinges. Whoever had caused the thumping was heading out of the house, not in. It wasn't his father.

He glanced at the old clock on his nightstand. The dim, orange glow showed that it was 10:30. Then he heard muffled voices as someone opened the front door again and made their way across the porch.

Joey tossed the covers aside and lowered his bare feet to the cold floorboards. A shiver ran through his body. He shrugged it off and tiptoed to the window. Drawing back the curtains a few inches, he peeked out.

Directly below his window, the snow-covered porch roof angled away from the house, cutting off his view of the porch steps and part of the driveway. But he could see Elizabeth's Bronco covered in six inches of fresh snow.

The Bronco's tailgate was open, the interior light shining. As Joey watched, Elizabeth emerged from under the porch roof and made her way to the back of her vehicle. There was a trampled path in the snow, so he knew this wasn't her first trip.

After quietly lifting a backpack into the back of the Bronco and sliding it forward, Elizabeth pulled out what Joey could see was the last of his mother's suitcases. Elizabeth set the suitcase on the path beside the Bronco's rear tire and swung the tailgate closed. Joey heard the faint click through the thin window glass, and the interior light winked out.

Joey's heart beat faster. Elizabeth was going somewhere, and she was keeping it secret. He had a bad feeling about this. Why would she be sneaking off in the middle of the night?

Just then, Miss Gortham emerged from under the porch roof carrying a bulging leather satchel, which she handed to Elizabeth.

Their whispered voices evoked farewells in Joey's mind. He couldn't make out the words, but he sensed this was a goodbye.

Joey was seized by a sudden urge to fly down the stairs and stop Elizabeth from leaving.

Don't go!

But he remained where he was, eyes focused on the scene below.

Miss Gortham hugged Elizabeth.

But where was Elizabeth going? Joey hadn't a clue. They were all supposed to drive up to Elizabeth's house in Morgantown tomorrow. But if that was the plan, then why did she take their luggage out of the car? It didn't make any sense.

Then a lightbulb flared in his mind, and he understood.

Ida.

Joey didn't want to lose his aunt. Elizabeth had been a safe harbor for him his whole life. But he also knew she and Ida were perfect for each other.

Wiping tears from his eyes, Joey watched as Miss Gortham stepped back from Elizabeth, then retrieved the suitcase from where it sat on the path.

"Goodbye, dear one. Be happy," Miss Gortham said.

Elizabeth climbed into the car and waved at Miss Gortham.

"Goodbye, my friend. Sweet Gigi, thank you for everything. I love you." Then Elizabeth backed down the driveway to the road before starting the engine.

As she did so, Elizabeth looked up at Joey's window. Joey's heart swelled. He flung the curtains wide and stood as close as he could to the glass, so his aunt could see him. He waved at her.

Elizabeth blew Joey a kiss. Then she turned her head, the brake lights went out, and the Bronco drove away, the snow crushing under its wheels.

Chapter 46

Rhonda woke from a restless night fraught with dreams of Max's rage. The snowstorm had passed during the night, the accumulation amounting to only six inches or so. Rhonda sat up in bed, disoriented. It took her a moment to realize she was in a bedroom at Miss Gortham's house. Liquid sunshine flooded through the windows into every corner of the room. She picked up her phone from the nightstand and checked the time. It was 8:30. She checked to see if she'd missed a call from the sheriff. She hadn't.

Rhonda climbed out of bed and wiped the sleep from her eyes. There was a comforting, low hum that she recognized as a forced air furnace, busy pumping warm air throughout the house. There were no other sounds. She expected to hear Elizabeth or Miss Gortham puttering around down in the kitchen, but other than the furnace the house was still.

"Guess I'm the first one up," she said, heading for the bathroom.

In the shower, hot water cascaded over her body.

Time will work it all out.

That was her mother's saying when Rhonda and Elizabeth were kids. It always frustrated her back then. She'd always wanted something more concrete. But now she smiled, knowing that her mother had been right. Time was working it out. And she was content to let it.

After toweling off, Rhonda checked her phone again—still no new message.

"Fine. Put it out of your mind," she said, as she pulled clothes from her suitcase and began to get dressed.

Rhonda descended the stairs and wandered into the living room.

"Is that you, dear," Miss Gortham called from the kitchen.

"Yes." Rhonda pushed through the swinging door and the aroma of fresh coffee hugged her in its saturating, glorious embrace.

Miss Gortham finished pouring a mug and handed it to Rhonda as she entered the kitchen.

"Here you are, dear."

"Thank you," said Rhonda. She liked her coffee strong and black, and this cup smelled like the most perfect cup ever brewed.

"Elizabeth is sleeping late," Rhonda noted. "She was always the first one up when we were young."

"Have a seat, dear," said Miss Gortham.

Something in the woman's tone chilled Rhonda's heart. She gripped her cup like a life preserver.

"Elizabeth is gone, dear."

Rhonda froze. She stared into her coffee cup. Miss Gortham laid a hand on Rhonda's shoulder and pointed to a large manilla envelope on the table.

"You'll come to understand her decision, in time, once the hurt has dulled."

Rhonda picked up the envelope. Her name was scrawled across the front in Elizabeth's hand. She unclasped the flap and pulled out the top sheet of paper. It was a letter to her, from her sister. She stared at it a moment and then read it.

My dearest Rhonda,

I can't tell you how happy it makes me, knowing you will be back in our childhood home! Knowing that you and Joey will be safe now.

I want you to always remember that I love you with all my heart. That has never changed and never will. You're my baby sister and now that I know you are safe, I can follow my own heart. Maybe you won't be able to understand, but I think, given a little time, you will.

I have been blinded by passion at the very thought of Ida since I first heard her name while conducting my research. Then meeting Georgina Gortham and reading Maggie's words about Ida only solidified my desire to know her even more. Georgina kept Maggie's letters too, ones that Ida had written her. There were only a few and I've kept those to myself. I know they were written to Maggie, not me, but the scope of her heart, her capacity for love, has left me breathless, my own heart aching.

I don't know how this works, or if it will at all. Maybe I'll wake up in the field with nothing but my own gullible stupidity for company. And if so, then I will see you soon! But if it works, as it did so dramatically in your case, then I hope you will wish me the happy life that I so much wish for you.

Maybe I'm insane, but I would never be happy again if I didn't at least try to reach her. Can you understand that?

I sincerely hope you can.

I've thought about this for a long time, ever since meeting Georgina. She set me on the path that led you to Ida's cabin. And with that success I have been unable to think of anything else. I have to try!

It is possible that this will work, and I'll arrive wherever Ida is, and we won't like each other. I don't think that's likely, but I have thought about it. But if it comes to that, at least we can be alone, together. Does that make sense?

I've fully transferred the house to your name. I know you will be happy there, and I love knowing that you and Joey will form loving memories there. You are both forever in my heart.

Be happy, sweet Rhonda!

I love you so much!

Please try to be happy for me.

Always, your loving sister,

Elizabeth

Rhonda sat motionless, the letter shaking softly in her trembling hand.

"No," she said.

"What, dear?"

"She wouldn't do this to me. Not after everything else that's happened. She wouldn't." Rhonda pushed her chair back and stood up.

Miss Gortham said nothing. She watched as Rhonda fled the kitchen.

"Elizabeth!" shouted Rhonda, as she ran toward the stairs. She saw her suitcases sitting side by side in the vestibule by the front door—they had been in Elizabeth's Bronco last night.

Running up the stairs, Rhonda pounded on Elizabeth's bedroom door.

"Elizabeth!" she shouted, a half choking sob escaping her throat.

There was no response.

"Elizabeth, please!"

"Mom!" called Joey from his room. His door flew open, and he hurried down the hall to where his mother stood staring into Elizabeth's empty room. "What's wrong?"

Chapter 47

Elizabeth scrambled through the dark. The snow had eased off and time was running out. She had until midnight, and it was almost that now. She covered her flashlight with a white cloth to mute the beam. She couldn't afford to be seen by the sheriff's deputy parked down the road.

Her nerves were on edge as she parted the bare branches blocking her way. And suddenly there it was!

Elizabeth stepped into the clearing, clutching the satchel to her chest. There were tangles of brambles, and tall dead grass, but no trees save for a few scrubby saplings. She could discern what she knew to be the remains of the cabin a hundred yards away, though nothing more than a jagged mound amid a jumble of snow-covered weeds gave them away. Here and there a few rotted logs stuck out like twigs from a nest, snow piling up on their charred surface. The tumbled chimney was recognizable, though its upper stones were scattered about on the ground. The lower eight feet stood solidly at the edge of the ruined cabin. The fireplace opening gaped a few feet above the ground where the floor must once have been.

She quickly covered the distance to the ruined structure. Once there, she shrugged off her backpack, leaned it against a foundation stone, unfastened the latch of the satchel strapped across her chest, and opened the flap. She unwrapped the cloth from her flashlight, the intensity of the released beam blinding her for a moment, and then she set it down in the trampled snow at her feet, its sharp beam casting skyward like a searchlight. With utmost care she withdrew the items from the bag and set about the task for which she'd so long prepared.

It has to work, she thought to herself. There was no room for doubt or second-guessing now. At last, it was time to finish this, her reward for her faith and perseverance.

Combining the gathered items, she struck a match and touched the flame to the nest of dried herbs. Praying with all of her academic heart, she hoped it would be enough. That it would indeed work. The flames flared and a green smoke drifted up through the beam of the flashlight.

Elizabeth carefully lifted the Mason jar of tea out of her bag. Then a sealed plastic sandwich bag. It contained a tiny pinch of herb. She opened the jar and placed it carefully on the snow.

Careful, careful, careful, she chanted in her mind.

Opening the plastic bag, she took a pinch of herbs and ground roots. Then she crumbled the herbs between her fingertips and sprinkled them into the jar and twisted the lid back on. Taking up the jar, she shook it vigorously. Satisfied it was mixed thoroughly, she removed the lid and lifted the jar to her lips and began to drink.

Grimacing at the bitter, foul taste, she suppressed a fit of coughing as the scratchy herbs caught in her throat. She finished the last of the potion and set the jar aside. She didn't feel anything at first, then her throat became numb, and her eyes started to droop.

Fatigue washed over her, and she laid down, using her backpack as a pillow, curling in the snow like a sleeping fawn. Around her, she became aware of a growing commotion in the trees, something swirling the air and thunderously stomping the ground. Then she drifted into a deep sleep, so deep that it bordered on death.

Elizabeth woke with a slight headache. She felt the strong rays of the sun on her face and heard birdsongs filling the air. And then she heard footsteps approaching her. She opened her eyes but the sun dazzled her at first.

A shadow appeared—someone was bending over her.

A woman, smiling sweetly, reached down, stroked Elizabeth's forehead, and said, "How are you feelin', honey?"

Chapter 48

"Come on, Joey, we have to go." Rhonda gripped Joey's arm, pulling him to the stairs.

"What's going on?" Joey broke free of his mother's grasp, but he still followed her down the stairs.

"Elizabeth is gone," shrieked Rhonda. She handed Joey his coat. "We have to stop her."

"I saw her leave last night," confessed Joey.

"You what?"

"She's gone to be with Ida. I think they'll be great together."

Rhonda stiffened.

"Mom?" Joey was worried.

Rhonda shook her head.

"Give her some time," said Miss Gortham who was now standing behind Joey.

Joey was startled.

"Come in the kitchen, Joey," said Miss Gortham.

"You knew, didn't you?" Rhonda asked.

"Yes," replied Miss Gortham. "I've known she would attempt to go there from the first time I met her."

"How could you let this happen?" Rhonda checked her anger. "I'm sorry, I don't understand. How is this even possible? I thought that the Teeka got what it wanted—that Ida would be able to die in peace."

"Well, yes," Miss Gortham said. "But not quite like you think. Ida has been trapped in a loop of sorts all these years. Awakened when a potentially worthy person finds their way to her, to act out the same routine to assess their suitability, and then, as has been the case every time until your husband, she simply winked out, back to sleep so to speak, until the next one.

"When Max was found acceptable, Ida was released from that loop. But she didn't die. She was released and left to live out her life on that little farm until her natural death."

"But, how? Was she returned to the time her cabin was burned? I don't understand."

"No, her original time has moved on, to our time now. When she drank the tea, she created her own separate pocket in the universe, separate from ours, where she was the sole human occupant, with the exception of the occasional visitor, such as yourself and Joey. Ida will live out her life there. And when she dies, that pocket in the universe that she created, will collapse back into this one, like it never existed."

Horror dawned on Rhonda's face. "What happens to Elizabeth then?"

"If she doesn't die first, she will return here, because that pocket is essentially of this world."

"How can she be returned? Didn't Ida die when she drank the tea? Didn't Elizabeth have to die too, to go there?" Rhonda's panic was rising.

Miss Gortham shook her head. "No. Ida died here when she drank the tea, because she had to open the pocket. She is only alive there. She cannot come back."

These words did nothing to sooth Rhonda's fear.

Miss Gortham smiled. "But the pocket was already there when Elizabeth went. She only had to drink a diluted tea to put her in a deep sleep after she summoned the Teeka. When you went over, you experienced a dizziness. Yes?"

Rhonda nodded. "Yes. Both when we first went and again when Max was chasing us through the woods. But we didn't drink any tea..." She stopped, remembering the tea Ida had made for them the morning before they left. "But we didn't drink anything before we arrived there in the first place."

"There was no need," said Miss Gortham. "Max was with you. The Teeka was waiting for him and had the pocket open for you to walk right in. Elizabeth went out to the cabin ruins the evening before and burned the herbs that summoned the Teeka so that it would be waiting for you."

The wall clock ticked away the moments.

"So, she'll come back," said Rhonda.

Rhonda's cell phone rang. She glanced at the screen and answered. "Yes?"

Rhonda listened to the caller, her eyes wide. A moment later she asked, "Where? Where is she?...Yes, we're still at Miss Gortham's house. I'm on my way. Thank you, sheriff." Rhonda slipped the phone back into her pocket. "Joey, we have to go."

"What's happening?"

"They found Max's body, something about a desiccated husk. I don't know. He's dead."

Joey didn't respond. Relief hit him like a tsunami.

"They found Elizabeth too!" Rhonda grabbed her coat and shrugged it on. "We have to go."

Rhonda stopped, then turned to Miss Gortham. "It seems I've forgotten that my car is still at the sheriff's station. Will you please drive us to the hospital in town?"

Chapter 49

The cold speared Max's body, and he shivered miserably. He was beginning to shut down. After waking in the forest, he climbed to his feet and staggered through the deep snow. He could find nothing that would help him get his bearings.

Where am I? *Nothing was familiar. Everything looked the same to his foggy mind. The frigid air sapped away his ability to think clearly.*

That means something, *he thought, though he couldn't grasp what it was.*

The last thing he remembered was chasing Rhonda, that fucking bitch, and his son, Joey, that little fucking faggot. *Then that roar descended, closing in from everywhere, and the woods went dark.* And the excruciating pain! OH MY GOD! *It seeped into every fiber of his body, as he felt himself coming apart, dissolving, being consumed. Max whimpered a desperate moan at the memory. And then there was nothing, and he woke up here.*

When was that? *He couldn't remember if it was today, or yesterday, or longer ago...He couldn't remember sleeping in the snow. His mind was fuzzy.*

Through the trees ahead, there was a clearing. The cabin, *he thought.* What else could it be? *He hurried as fast as his stiff, clumsy legs could carry him. Which wasn't fast at all. The deep snow froze his skin, working its way under his pant cuffs and down his socks. His frozen jeans were stiff in the frigid air, and he could feel the skin on his legs numbing, beginning to freeze. He blinked his eyes rapidly at the ice crusting his lashes, searching for something familiar—somewhere he could go to escape the bitter cold.*

Standing at the edge of the forest, he saw the familiar clearing. But there was no cabin. The clearing, which he held no doubt was the same one he and his family had stumbled into, was empty of any sign of human habitation. There was no cabin, or barn, or chicken house, not even the outhouse!

"WHAT THE FUCK!" he screamed at the top of his lungs. His throat was raw from the cold, grating air.

Panic took hold. His breath came in short spastic bursts as he spun around, his mind desperate to locate where he'd made his mistake. *It just looks like the same place.* But even in his disorientation, he knew it wasn't so. He knew it was the same place. He recognized certain trees, the one with the rotten spot where a branch had blown off over near where the barn should be. There were two pine trees, like sentries, where they'd first emerged from the woods, searching for the light they'd seen through the trees, and later where he'd chased his family.

Max didn't know how long he'd been standing there trying to force the scene before him to change. But it refused, and now his face was numb. He couldn't feel his nose, even when he raised a hand and touched it. And he couldn't feel his fingers either. His cheeks felt like blocks of ice clumped onto his skull. His lips were cracked and oozing blood.

A sobering shot of adrenaline jolted him as he suddenly remembered what he'd been trying to think of; Hypotherm...! Hypo...? Hyper...? The word floated away, but its meaning lodged in his mind. He was fucked if he couldn't find someplace to get out of the cold. The sky was a flat covering of gray clouds. As he stared up at them, hoping they could point him in the direction he needed to go, snow began to flutter down. Slowly at first, and then steadily increasing to a thick veil of white, landing on his frozen upturned face.

"No, no, no," he chanted through numb lips as he stumbled down what should have been the narrow lane between the forest and the zigzagging fence. But it wasn't really a lane now because there was no fence to define it. Max thought this was terribly funny. A choked, wheezing laugh erupted from his throat before quickly evolving into a desperate cough that threatened to seize his lungs.

The car! *If he could just find his way through the forest to his car, he would be fine.* The coughing subsided, but his mind was becoming thick, clouded. He absently patted his coat pocket—his key fob was missing. *The bitch took it.* His frustration was growing. He trudged through the snow with a single-minded train of thought. *The car was stuck. They couldn't leave him. They would still be sitting there.*

So cold! "So fffuuucking cold," *he whispered, but wasn't sure if he'd said it or only thought it. He had no idea how long he'd been out here in this frozen wasteland.* Was I asleep? *He thought he remembered waking up, partially buried in crusty snow. So that must mean he'd spent the night out here, didn't it? But that wasn't right, was it? It was daylight, morning, when they left Ida's cabin. When they were in the woods, right before that thing attacked him, it had been night. How could that be? His mind insisted that he was mistaken.*

Even as his face and extremities froze, sweat soaked his back beneath his coat, the last vestige of heat in his body seeping away. He could feel the thrumming cold working through the fabric and freezing his shirt to his skin. Fuck! Fuck! Fuck! *He stumbled in the thigh-deep snow. He face-planted into a drift. Shocking cold burned his eyes and clogged his mouth as he tried to inhale.*

GET UP! *His mind screamed at him. His brain frantically signaled his arms and legs to lift him up. But his freezing muscles refused to respond, the receptors numb and dying.*

Managing to roll onto his side, Max twisted his neck enough to turn his head away from the snow blocking his breath. He gasped and sucked in gulps of freezing air, his throat turning to fire. Violent coughing erupted from his lungs. His heart pounded like a racing engine in his chest.

Moaning, Max turned back to the way he had come. The empty field lay quiet and still. His brain quieted, and thoughts of his wife and son were gone. Thoughts of escaping this nightmare evaporated. Really, now that he was cuddled in the snowbank, it wasn't so bad. He couldn't feel his extremities anymore, but a general feeling of warmth began to flow through him, like a hot spring welling from the ground, and Max wondered if he might be saved after all. Someone would come looking for him eventually. A general conviction that his wife—he couldn't remember her name just now but was sure it would come to him—would send someone. Send someone to do what? He didn't know, couldn't remember what the question was. Had he fallen asleep again?

It's getting so hot! Max struggled with all his strength. He managed to fling his arms back and forth and shrug his coat partially off his body. Then his arms became entangled, like a loose straitjacket binding him in the stiff fabric. He gave up after a moment or two, unable to coax any more movement from his body. He couldn't remember what he was trying to do anyway. He couldn't tell if he was still hot anymore either. He couldn't remember anything. His heart was slowing—a sputtering motor after the key had been switched off. His breathing was shallow and slowing too.

Max didn't notice when the snow stopped falling. But he questioned the sky darkening so quickly. But when the stomping surged around him, he realized he was being invaded again by the stinging hordes. He tried to scream. But there was no sound. The darkness was complete. There was only the pain of his body being devoured. His blood and organs and muscle tissue dissolved and voided into the darkness, as he felt the horror of being eaten alive from the inside out.

Max woke in a drift of snow, again. The deserted forest around him was a scene of deep winter. He rolled over, his limbs frozen.

"What the fuck?"

This can't be happening again!

But it was, and would again and again, for as long as Ida lived, only ending the horrible cycle when she died her natural death, and the Teeka finally consumed the last of his bitter essence.

Chapter 50

Miss Gortham nodded. "Yes, Rhonda, I'd be happy to take you to see Elizabeth in the hospital."

"Thank you," said Rhonda, zipping up her coat and rushing out the front door.

Miss Gortham lay her hand on Joey's shoulder. "Prepare yourself, dear. I don't think your mother's going to find what she's hoping for."

Joey started to reply but Miss Gortham shook her head.

Miss Gortham parked the car near the emergency entrance to the small, rural hospital. The sheriff's car was parked nearby. Rhonda leapt out and hurried inside. Joey and Miss Gortham followed her.

Looking around the small waiting area, Rhonda spied the sheriff coming out of the treatment area.

"Sheriff!" she called.

The sheriff looked up. "Mrs. Ingram, I'm so sorry about your husband. We'll need you to identify the body to be sure it's him, but he had his wallet. I don't think there's any doubt. I can't explain what could have done that to him..."

"Thank you, sheriff," said Rhonda. Max was dead, good. She wanted to see her sister. "Where is Elizabeth? Can I see her? Is she all right?"

The questions spewed out.

The sheriff opened the door to the ward. "She's in there. You should prepare yourself."

"For what?" asked Rhonda.

"We found her Bronco pulled over about a quarter mile from the end of the road, where my deputy had been parked overnight. When he found it, he followed her tracks through the woods and spotted her in the field near the old cabin ruins. She was kneeling in the snow by a gravestone."

Rhonda stopped short. "What gravestone? Whose grave?"

"The name *Ida* was scratched on the stone," said the sheriff. "Your sister was crying and didn't realize my deputy was there. She resisted when he started to lead her away, but her strength was nearly gone. I'm sorry to say, she's in a pretty bad way. She was out in the cold for quite a while. The doctor says she likely won't last much longer."

Miss Gortham's words echoed through Rhonda's mind, and something clicked into place. She heard a *zing* as Joey drew the curtain open.

There was a moment of quiet, the beeps and buzzing of hospital machines fading into the background. Then Joey's strained, frightened voice called to her. "Mom?"

As Rhonda stood at the foot of the bed, she cupped her hands over her mouth as if she were stifling a scream that threatened to explode. But there was no scream. When she looked at the woman in the bed, she knew instantly that it was her sister, Elizabeth. Tears flowed as she made her way around the foot of the bed. Joey was in shock, his eyes riveted on the woman.

Rhonda took Elizabeth's withered hand in her own. "Oh, Elizabeth." Rhonda squeezed the frail, callused hand of her sister. Then she asked in a gentle, hopeful voice, "Was it worth it?"

Elizabeth locked her gaze on Rhonda with rheumy, cloudy, but keenly alert eyes. The skin of her age-withered face crinkled as she smiled, her thin, gray hair unkempt and wild.

"Oh, yes!" Her voice was an ancient croak, diminished by decades of wood smoke and harsh winter air, and yet youthful in its enthusiasm. A few tears worked their way down her cheek, like a spring down a craggy cliff. She squeezed Rhonda's hand.

"There was time after Ida died, before the world closed. I got to bury her before the dark came."

Rhonda broke down and cried.

Miss Gortham looked in on her friend. Elizabeth's eyes met hers with a brief mischievous sparkle.

She must be in her seventies now, thought Rhonda.

She sat with her sister, holding her hand. Joey pulled up a chair and sat next to his mother, resting his head on her shoulder. They sat there together for an hour, before Elizabeth finally slipped away, a contented smile etched on her wrinkled face.

"I love you," Rhonda said, leaning over and kissing her sister's forehead.

The sheriff returned and put his hand on Rhonda's shoulder. "I'm so sorry for your loss."

Rhonda nodded, her eyes drifting back to Elizabeth's lifeless form on the bed.

Epilogue

Ida knelt on the sun-warmed ground in her garden, savoring the fresh, loamy scent of the newly turned earth. She looked up at the crystal clear sky; so impossibly blue it nearly blinded her with its beauty, so deep she could swim in it. She moved along the row, gently depositing a seed in each hole she made with her finger.

Chickens happily clucked in their pen, vigorously digging and pecking at the ground for insects to eat. Oats and Sugar grazed on fresh spring grass nearby. A gentle warm breeze carried the heavenly sweet scent of chamomile from the patch Ida kept at the corner of the field.

"Oh, that's lovely," she said, lifting her nose into the breeze to more fully catch the aroma. She'd waited so long for the day she could see her land come back to life again, the long, long winter ended at last.

She heard the squeak of the front door opening, and the footsteps on the porch floorboards of the cabin. She twisted to look back over her shoulder, a broad smile creasing her face, her eyes sparkling in delight.

Elizabeth's warm voice called out from the porch, "Ida?"

Ida smiled and replied, "Yes, my love! Come and join me!"

Acknowledgments

Thank you to my husband, best friend, and first reader, Chuck Walker. Your love, support, and understanding mean the world to me. I love you with all my heart.

A huge thank you to Eric Peterson for your wholehearted endorsement of this book and for your efforts to help me get it published. Larry Rosen, thank you for your candor and enthusiasm, and continued willingness to read my stories. Thank you, Maureen Thomas, for your honesty—it spurred a necessary—and fruitful—critical look at my writing. To my mother, Elizabeth Anne Reed, and my sister, Rebecca Elizabeth Reed-Fitzpatrick, thank you for the encouraging feedback that rekindled my sputtering spark of confidence.

Thank you to the folks at Rattling Good Yarns Press; publisher Ian Henzel for that glorious word, "Yes"; and editor-extraordinaire St Sukie de la Croix for providing an unwavering, insightful guiding hand in editing this book.

About the Author

Michael Reed grew up in Maryland and Colorado. His grandmother, Anne Louise Smith-Sylvester, instilled in Michael his great love for nature, history, folklore, and above all else, reading. In his early twenties Michael pulled on his backpack and moved to Alaska, where he lived for over a decade. He worked at Denali National Park, commercial fished in Cook Inlet, attended Kenai Peninsula College, built a log cabin, and raised and mushed sled dogs. Michael now lives in West Virginia with his husband of twenty years, and their dog, Cody. When he's not working on his next novel, reading, or building custom furniture—from lumber he mills himself, he continues work on the house he began building fourteen years ago. *Desperate Measures* is his first published work.

Author, Michael Reed